Dark Blue Death

Dark Blue Death

A Zoe Barrow Mystery

Jan Grape

Five Star • Waterville, Maine

First Edition
First Printing: November 2005

Published in 2005 in conjunction with Tekno Books
and Ed Gorman.

Set in 11 pt. Plantin by Elena Picard..

Printed in the United States on permanent paper.

Library of Congress Cataloging-in-Publication Data

Grape, Jan.
    Dark blue death : a Zoe Barrow mystery / by Jan Grape.
    —1st ed.
        p. cm.
        ISBN 1-59414-423-0 (hc : alk. paper)
        1. Police—Texas—Austin—Fiction. 2. Nursing
home patients—Fiction. 3. Missing persons—Fiction.
4. Police murders—Fiction. 5. Austin (Tex.)—Fiction.
6. Policewomen—Fiction. I. Title.
PS3607.R373D37 2005
    813′.6—dc22   2005024280

Dedication

In Memory of Barbara Burnett Smith Petry

In Memory of Bill Hagemeier

In Memory of APD Commander Shauna Jacobson, who walked the walk and talked the talk.

Acknowledgments

◆ ◆ ◆

To Commander Shauna Jacobson whose untimely death in December leaves a big heartache in APD. To Detective Linda Cooper Everwijn, great friend, reader, and answerer of questions. To Sergeant Jessica Robledo, APD Homicide for fantastic help, answers, and insights. To Tello Leal, for Victim's Services information. To Anne Petrochelli, APD for "war stories," and a fun day of role-play. To the Citizen's Police Academy Alumni aka Grambo's Chicks for inspiration. To the North Rim, Grand Canyon, AZ crew for name inspirations. To Bill Hagemeier for help on Yamahas & computer advice. To Tom Cole regarding funeral home procedures. To Jesse Sublett for info on the Sixth street music scene. To Art Torres of Taos, NM for the tattoo idea. To Ed Gorman who keeps me from discouragement. To Susan Cooper for reading, editing, and expert advice. To my husband Elmer Grape, for great support, suggestions, and expert advice. Any mistakes or errors in information are definitely mine. Although real names have been used on occasion, the characters are all fictional and any resemblance to real people, living or dead is entirely coincidental.

Author's Note

◆ ◆ ◆

AUSTIN, TEXAS

Austin's Police Chief oversees an agency with more than 1,300 officers, over 500 civilian employees and a current budget of 155 million dollars.

Prologue

He turned off the asphalt road and stopped on the steep driveway. He always thought this house was perfect except for this stupid driveway. Sometimes he almost didn't have the energy to roll his new YZF-R1 to a stop and push on the kickstand at the same time. He punched in the code and the garage door opened easily. He hurriedly rolled the Yamaha into the garage and closed the door. It wasn't until he was inside, locked up and secure that he let out the breath he'd subconsciously been holding.

Nasty. Dir . . . ty.

Unzipping and removing his boots, he stripped off the leather leggings. The shirt, T-shirt, and underwear followed. Everything went into its proper place and he stepped into the shower, and got totally wet then covered his body with the sanitizing soap. He used the body brush and the loofah, scrubbing, and exfoliating. After adding shaving soap, he removed the razor's top and shaved; his head, underarms, pubic area, stomach, and chest. Then once more he ran the loofah over his body.

Disgusting and filthy.

He rinsed with lukewarm water and turned the faucet until the water grew cold and colder, then let it splash all over his body closing the pores.

He stepped out, shivering, and opened a big, white,

heated cotton towel and dried. Afterwards he looked at his body thoroughly in the full-length mirror.

He turned and inspected the facial scars, the longest one running from his left eyebrow and down along the left cheekbone. He squinted and tried to blur out the misshapen one. Need some drops to get the red out, he thought.

He couldn't help the one quick peek in the mirror at the jagged scar across the groin, but he hated looking at it and focused instead on the wall.

"Don't touch yourself there. You dirty boy. I'll cut you if I see you doing that again," he heard the words in his head.

It took a few minutes but soon the tension left as the residue of the day finally drained away. The timer on the light switch clicked off. He reached inside the cabinet and pulled on a pair of fresh, cool underwear. Before leaving the bathroom, he opened the small bottle of magnesia pills and popped three, washing them down with bottled water.

He was quite pleased when he entered the kitchen and noted the time. "Eighteen minutes. A new personal best."

You nasty, dirty boy. You evil son of Satan.

"Nasty, dirty. Oohh, nas . . . ty," he said aloud, looking at the nude woman on the computer screen. Mother would have a stroke if she saw this slut—if she was still alive—he chuckled. That pitiful and timid little woman who had given him birth was only a dim memory but her favorite expressions rang in his head: "That's nasty. Don't touch yourself there. You're nasty." He remembered hearing her day and night, night and day. Funny, he thought, I still can hear her sometimes.

He kept clicking the mouse, watching nude photos change, realizing these women were truly sluts. Pop would have enjoyed them though. They are just asking for it when they post these nasty pictures on the Internet for everyone

10

to see. He clicked the mouse again and again letting their private parts fill the huge screen, in living color.

He felt his body betray once again. He made a fist and pounded his groin. "Go way. You can't come out to play now, you nasty boy." He closed the photo site and put the computer in standby mode.

He walked quickly into the kitchen, grabbed a handful of Oreo cookies out of the pantry, and poured a glass of milk. After eating, he walked back to his computer and sat down in front of his monitor.

But now there is one less slut to dirty up the world, he thought as he brought the computer screen back to life.

Citizen Police Academy

The Citizen Police Academy was established in January 1987 and more than 1,400 citizens have graduated from 51 classes.

The Citizen Police Academy is a twelve-week program designed to give the public a working knowledge of the Austin Police Department. Each session consists of twelve consecutive Tuesday night classes held at Austin Police Department Facilities from 6:00 p.m. to 10:00 p.m. The instruction is comprehensive and each week separate areas of the department are covered.

Training, communication, canine, patrol, S.W.A.T., and recruiting are examples of some of the topics that are covered. Instruction consists of lectures, demonstrations, tours, and riding with a police officer on a ten-hour shift.

The slogan of the Citizen Police Academy is "Understanding through Education." The goal is to provide enough information to the public to dispel misconceptions and to increase the rapport between citizens and police officers.

We hope the graduates of the Citizen Police Academy become more aware and better informed about how the Police Department operates, and will recommend their friends, coworkers and families to join the Austin Police Department in this rewarding program. (Austin City Connection - The Official Web site of the City of Austin)

Chapter One

◆　◆　◆

"Those two were a couple of wussies," I said to Anne. "I expected them to wash out before now." The sun beat down on the white SUV sitting on the black asphalt of the defensive driving course at the Austin Police Academy. The September heat and humidity caused both Anne and I to glow. Yes, it's true. Southern women don't sweat—they glow. However, a bit of a breeze wafted through the windows occasionally and cooled that glow just the same as if it were sweat.

"I agree," Anne replied. "But role-play will give us an idea if they have the right stuff or not." Her mouth hinted at a slightly evil smile. "If we do a good enough acting job in this role-play they'll forget we're training them. And it's better that we catch their slip-ups now. If they goof out on the street they might get dead."

During role-play, there are people who act or pretend to be lawbreakers and/or crooks and the cadets must deal with that particular scenario. These role-playing scenarios are set up in a particular way so that the cadets interact with the actors as if these were actual perpetrators. A field-training officer observes the scene and then critiques each cadet on how they handled the crime, the perp, the interaction, the arrest if necessary, and then the cadets are instructed on how they might improve their handling of the problem. If the actors are good enough, everyone, including the cadet forgets this is play-acting and reacts in an honest way. Sometimes the cadet overreacts or even goes off on the actor-crook and the training officers need to know this, too. Psychologically testing them, if you will.

Anne Panzarella is a sergeant and one of the teaching/training officers at the Academy and a longtime friend of mine. We both had worked patrol, narcotics and fraud about the same time. Blonde and green-eyed, she stood three inches below my five feet nine but carried herself in a way that made her seem closer to my height. She exercised regularly and amazed me with her strength.

In her off time, she captained a championship softball team. She has been married to the same guy for fifteen years—a minor miracle among police officers. The fact that he, too was in law enforcement was most likely the reason. In our world it's difficult to find an understanding man when you're working the graveyard shift, or on an all-night stakeout with another officer who happens to be male. Only another cop can know and understand why you're mad at the world when the judge throws your case out and the scumbag walks.

Anne had been one of the first women in APD, but her advancement had been slow because she often was too out-spoken. Office politics often demanded a lot of "go along, get along." She never subscribed to that theory. But seniority now worked in her favor, and I could only be pleased for her.

My boss, Commander Lianne Crowder, volunteered me for four weeks at the police academy as a field training officer and I didn't protest. It was a good way to get acquainted with this batch of FNGs (fucking new guys) and refresh my own skills along the way. At this point in their training, the cadets had only had classroom and book learning. Now it was time to learn mundane things: how to drive a patrol car, how to operate the siren, the lights, and the computer, how to speak coherently over a walkie-talkie, and most important of all, how to keep up with all their paper work. Now they would get a glimmer of what it would actually be like to be a police officer in Austin, Texas.

The department built a complex for the academy on the far edge of town in the southeastern part of the county. The main building housed offices, a kitchen, some classrooms, and a small exercise room. A larger classroom building sat to one side, and the indoor firing range completes the complex. Behind and to one side of the buildings is a paved area for driver's training and other moving violation and traffic stops. An area is set aside for SWAT team training that's in back, and around on the side of the main building is another paved area and the fire academy's training tower.

The cadets who were in training now had all talked for weeks about how much crime they were going to solve. Each of them thought they were going to make detective first trip out. The routine of traffic and neighborhood patrol sounded much too boring when you were twenty-something. They were so full of piss and vinegar it actually made me tired watching them.

"Zoe-y? Here's the other two I was talking about. Nottingham and Sanchez."

Anne knew how to pronounce my name (rhyming with Joe), but could never help teasing me, knowing I could sometimes get testy about it. I gave it back to her though, often calling her Mozzarella instead of Panzarella. I checked the rearview mirror and watched the two cadets approaching from behind our vehicle. "Oh yes, I remember them now. She's Miss Milquetoast. And he's one of those cocky know-it-alls."

"You got 'em nailed. They're about as close to washouts as you can get. Role-play will be a big factor in my deciding if they make it or not."

The scenario called for the cadets to pretend to have made a non-felony traffic stop on the violators—Anne and myself—who just ran a stop sign. The lead cadet, in this case, Cadet Robert Nottingham, would question Anne as she had been driving. During the questioning, if he did it correctly, he would discover Anne didn't have her car insurance card with her.

Actually I, as Anne's passenger, had her insurance card in my purse and could produce it. But we wanted to see how they would handle the situation in every aspect. See if Nottingham would ask for each item needed and also obtain the card from me. Cadet Ramona Sanchez, as backup, would be standing a few feet from the passenger side door where I was sitting. Her job mainly consisted of looking into the passenger side to be sure I didn't have a gun or anything suspicious in sight. And checking out the back seat in case there was a third suspicious passenger.

"Ma'am?" said Nottingham, to Anne. "May I see your driver's license?"

"What did I do wrong, officer?" said Anne.

"You ran that stop sign back there."

"No, I didn't. Did I run that stop sign, Zoe?"

"Hell, no. You stopped," I chimed in.

"Ma'am. I need to see your license."

Anne slowly picked up her purse, got out her license, and handed it to him. She put a huge wad of bubble gum into her mouth and began chewing loudly, then reached and turned up the volume to the radio.

The cadet on my side, Miss Sanchez, did nothing except stand there, looking bored. Anne glanced over at Sanchez and rolled up the window on the passenger side. Sanchez frowned but didn't say a word. She just stood there, trying to look fierce with her hand lightly touching the wooden gun in her holder. You don't think we'd issue real guns to them yet, do you?

Nottingham, voice rising to be heard over the loud music, asked for Anne's driver's license and insurance. Anne handed him her license.

Nottingham looked at her license, then said, "I still need your proof of insurance."

Anne turned to me, "Zoe, you've got my insurance card, don't you?"

"I don't think so, girlfriend."

"Remember? Last night when you borrowed my car, and I made you put my insurance card in your purse so you could find it if you needed it."

"Oh, yeah," I said and started digging in my purse after the card.

Looking at her license and his ticket book, Nottingham began asking Anne questions. "Is this your current address, ma'am? And ma'am would you please turn down the radio?"

"Yes, it is." Anne turned the radio down a bit. But only a smidgen.

"And what is your occupation?" Nottingham made his notes in his ticket book, filling in all the blanks. His routine was strictly by the book.

"I'm a telephone sex operator."

Anne couldn't see Nottingham, he was standing a bit behind her left shoulder, but I could see him in the rearview mirror perfectly. He was writing in his little ticket book

17

when Anne said she was a phone sex operator. He continued writing for a moment, then sort of did a double take when her words sunk in, his eyes rolled up and met mine in the mirror and he tried unsuccessfully to suppress a laugh. It came out a cough.

"You got a problem with what I do, young man?"

"Uh, no, ma'am. Not at all." His voice strangled.

"Good."

"And ma'am, may I have your phone number, ma'am?"

"Why? You gonna call me?"

"Uh, no, ma'am. It's just for my records."

Anne turned to me. "Hey, Zoe. This hanky cop wants to call me."

"Little young for you, ain't he?"

"Get 'em young and train 'em right, I always say." We both laughed more than the old joke called for, but we were having fun with it all.

"Ma'am?" Nottingham said. "Your phone number?"

"I'll give you my work number."

"That's fine, ma'am."

"It's 1-800-GOOD SEX."

By this time Nottingham is almost having convolutions. Sanchez, who is in the dark from this merriment, still stands with one hand on her gun, and is obviously bored to tears.

Anne looked at me and said just loud enough for me to hear, "I love to mess with their heads. They're not expecting a hard time from us. They think we'll act in some pre-programmed routine way."

We both knew real people never acted like a textbook case and it was something the cadets needed to learn right now before they got on the street. While Anne had Nottingham rattled, I decided to shake up Sanchez, too.

18

"Watch this," I said to Anne as I opened the passenger door.

Cadet Sanchez backed up a little, held her hands up to halt me, and said, "Stay in the car, ma'am." She was a slender woman, but wiry, and looked to be in pretty good shape. The academy had exercise equipment and most of the FNGs utilized it. Her dark brown hair was pulled back tight into a ponytail that caused her brown eyes to bulge a bit.

"Y'all are taking too damn long here and I gotta go to the bathroom. I'm going over there to that Shamrock station restroom." There was no service station around, it was part of my play-acting scene.

"Ma'am, you need to stay in your car. We won't be much longer." Sanchez's quiet voice held only a lilting accent. Unless she learned to speak up she'd never be believable as a cop. Get her out to kick open a door, yelling "POLICE," and no one behind that door would hear her or care to respond to the order.

"Well, too bad. I'm not going to wet my pants just because you need to make your ticket quota and you take all day doing it."

Anne turned down the radio. "You'd better let her go. She's got a bladder problem, and I don't want my leather seats ruined." I stomped off down the sidewalk, mimicking Anne's voice, *"I don't want my leather seats ruined,"* then muttering, "as if I would do such a thing and how dare she tell the world I have a bladder problem."

Sanchez began to stutter, "But . . . bu—"

Anne called out "Cut" for the scenario. I walked back to the car as Anne opened her car door and stood ready to ream out Sanchez for letting me go and Nottingham for being so crude as to laugh at her occupation. She'd also bust his chops for not ever getting the insurance card from me.

And so that's the way it went for the next hour or so.

We don't often get such nice days in September in Central Texas. More often than not, the heat is unbearable. Cooler weather usually didn't arrive here until December. The temperature today hovered in the low eighties with some humidity but also with a light cooling breeze. Big fluffy clouds and a sky so blue it hurt your eyes. A perfectly nice day to be outdoors, even if we were working.

Anne and I both wore knee-length denim shorts and cotton T-shirts. It only took a person one summer to learn that cotton was cooler in Texas. My shorts were tan and my shirt light green. Anne wore blue jean shorts and a white shirt. We both also wore sneakers. It's amazing how everyone from oldsters to babies wear sneakers 99 percent of the time. Great for comfort and if you paid a little more for them, they were long lasting. Thing is most of us get tired of the same shoes all the time so we wind up buying several pairs. I love the fact that they now have gold lamé and sequined ones you can wear for dress-up occasions.

While waiting for each new twosome to arrive, Anne kept me in stitches with war stories of back when she first joined the police department. As one of the first female officers in Austin, people would even stop their car just to stare at her when she worked patrol. "I'd have my hair back in a ponytail and with my hat on (it was mandatory we wear our hats back then) I looked like a short guy. I'd walk up to a car, and if there was a female driver, it could get funny. I'd ask for her license in as deep a voice as I could manage. While she's reaching in her purse I'd take off my hat and when she turned, all smiles ready to flirt her way out of a ticket, her face would fall when she saw a female officer standing there."

I laughed and Anne continued.

"I learned the 'gotta go to the bathroom scam' during my first month on the street," Anne said. "I was by myself one day, riding traffic and stopped a pregnant woman. She asked permission to go to the service station restroom just a few feet from where we were stopped. I had her driver's license in my hand and knowing pregnant women had bladder control problems, told her 'sure.' But she boogied."

"She ran out on you?"

"Yep, and I had to go back and tell my sergeant that I'd lost her. Took a long time to live that one down. From that point on, if someone tried to pull the bathroom business with me, I'd tell 'em, fine. I'll go with you. And sometimes I had to do it because they really had to go, but when that happened, then I'd stand outside the door and wait on them."

"Hard lessons, but we learned, didn't we?" I said. Someone had mentioned the bathroom trick to me so I never lost one that way.

She nodded.

"I remember one time my first week," I said. "I was riding with Earl Rodman. You remember Earl? He died last year. Heart, I think. So sad, his wife died about a year before that and he was never the same. He and I were running radar out on Interstate 35 out near Highland Mall. A cute little co-ed in a Mustang convertible went by and I clocked her at seventy-five miles per hour. We took off after, got her stopped and Earl got out and walked over to her car while I called in her license plates. He was back in about thirty seconds, and I saw that Mustang pulling out and leaving.

" 'What's with that?' I asked him. 'She just started her period,' he says 'and was hurrying home.' I said, 'Earl, she

21

got you. Look, women start their periods every day, so big deal. Don't let them pull that crap on you.' Then he says, 'She offered to show me and started pushing her skirt higher and higher. I thought I'd better get out of there before things got hinky. So I told her to take off.'

"That's when I clued him that the co-ed had truly got to him. The old raising the skirt trick can work with guys. Unless of course they do want to see the wares, and then she can report him for conduct unbecoming." Anne and I laughed and both said "Men," at the same time.

It felt good to laugh and be relaxed with a fellow officer. I'd had a rough time after shooting a bad guy. Nothing anyone can say or do to make you feel any better. Even though this guy deserved to die. He had pistol-whipped a convenience store clerk during a robbery, shot one police officer in the abdomen while fleeing, and took another police officer hostage, also shooting her in the hand.

Even now, thinking about it could give me cold chills. I had been off-duty at the time, heading home after a basketball game but had heard the call over the radio that an officer was down, and since I was nearby, I had responded.

The location of the action was the old Palmer Auditorium. When I arrived I'd found fellow officer Lopez sitting on the ground by his squad car. A pool of blood was around him and his radio microphone dangled in the air beside him.

He told me another officer, a young woman named Ticer, had followed the creep inside. As I sat with Lopez hoping like crazy that he wouldn't die right before my eyes, I heard a shot fired. Coming from the auditorium's lower level.

I knew backup was on the way, but I couldn't let Officer Ticer down if she wasn't already dead. I made my way down the stairs and into the exhibit room.

I located the guy in the shadowy gloom and saw that the gunman had a chokehold on Ticer and when I told him, "Police. Give it up," he threw Ticer down and fired at me. I returned his fire and in only moments, I was standing over him. I'd killed a young man who in death looked little more than a schoolboy. But he wasn't innocent. Not only had he wounded Officer Ticer and Lopez, I found out he was Jesse Garcia. The gangbanger who had shot my husband, SWAT Officer Byron Barrow, and left him in a vegetative state.

The shooting of Byron, had been, in reality, accidental, but Garcia had been a gangbanger fighting a turf war who'd had no business firing a gun at anyone.

"Anne, have you ever had to shoot anyone?" I asked, although I knew the answer.

"No. But I came close to it several times." She turned to me and said, "Zoe. You did what had to be done. You can't keep dwelling on the shooting. It will eat your lunch if you do."

"In my head I know you're right, but sometimes in my heart, I can't stop thinking about it."

"You wouldn't be human otherwise. Are you still in counseling?"

"Not on a regular basis anymore. When things get bad, I see Doc Morton." Morton was our police shrink. I'd had to talk to him immediately after I'd shot Garcia. It was mandatory in an officer involved shooting. "When things get really bad, I have a couple of drinks. Most of the time, I'm okay."

"From everything I've heard, I think you're doing good." Anne cleared her throat. "I don't usually talk about it, but Doc Martin helped me when my first husband walked out on me."

I had no idea Anne had been married before, but I wasn't surprised either. Divorce rate among police officers is very high. "Doc is the best," I said.

"Believe me, these lousy feelings over the shooting will get easier with time. I know that's a cliché but it honestly *is* true," Anne said.

"I know. Yet sometimes in the mornings when I wake up and think about Garcia's dead body lying there, I have to keep telling myself over and over that it was him or me. Him or me."

"That's about the only way you can keep your sanity."

Suddenly, I heard feet pounding on the asphalt behind me, we turned and saw Nottingham running towards us. Anne and I both jumped out of her SUV to meet him.

"What's wrong?"

Nottingham, his face pasty, breath coming hard and fast, said "It's Sanchez. She's been shot and she's dead. And Sergeant Torres told me to come and get Ms. Barrow."

"Aw, no," I said, "Where?" And started running alongside him. Anne trailed behind as she had to grab the walkie-talkie out of her car before following.

"In the classroom, near the shooting range."

"Oh, shit, don't tell me one of our own guys shot her," I said.

Citizen Police Academy—
Frequently Asked Questions

What is the purpose of conducting a citizen police academy?

To give the public information on how the Police Department works and its policies and procedures, through a series of classes involving instruction by police officers.

Where did the concept originate?

The program originated in Orlando, Florida in 1984. Orlando was the first city in the United States to start a Citizen Police Academy.

What was the Austin Police Department's incentive for starting a Citizen Police Academy?

We feel the more information the public has about the police department, less fears and misconceptions will exist. Many conflicts are caused simply by lack of understanding.

When does the class meet?

There are three Citizen Police Academy sessions per year. Students meet on Tuesday nights at different Austin Police Department facilities. There will be a total of approximately thirty-five (35) hours of instruction by police officers. The classes are held at no cost to the student!

Who attends the Citizen Police Academy?

Students range from 17 years of age and above. We have architects, bankers, homemakers, students, retirees, teachers, neighborhood groups, and professionals attending the classes.

(Austin City Connection -
The Official Web site of the City of Austin)

Chapter Two

I couldn't believe my eyes when I arrived at the scene. At least twenty people surrounded the body of Cadet Ramona Sanchez. "Freeze. Everybody freeze," I said. Forty or so pairs of eyes looked at me like I was nuts. "You idiots are messing up a crime scene. You training officers should know better."

"Sorry, Zoe," said Sergeant Torres. "I bent over to check for a pulse but didn't touch anything else."

Torres was a highly competent officer, currently on medical leave. He had been on traffic patrol over the Fourth of July weekend. While he was writing a ticket for speeding, a car sideswiped him. Torres wound up with a broken ankle and a concussion. Unfortunately, the ankle was slow to heal so Torres was teaching at the academy. The driver of the car who had hit Torres had been driving under the influence, but he had been caught, and his trial was due to start in a month or so.

"Make a hole," someone said.

"Don't you dare. Nobody move." The first time I heard that expression it sounded like they were saying, "Make a whore." Instead, they were wanting everyone to quickly stand to one side and allow passage without having to wait for someone who might be in the way. They did it for anyone, male, female, civilian, officers.

"Everybody stay right where they are *NOW!*

"Good. Now everyone step back—twelve paces—directly in back of where you are so you don't contaminate anyplace else." They moved back in unison. I hoped they'd stayed sort of in their same path and didn't add any more contamination.

"Have you called communication?" I asked Torres. The communication supervisor was the first contact to be made. I realized we had a big problem here without the proper personnel to handle things.

"Yes, ma'am," Art Torres said. "I called on my cell phone." He rubbed his eyes with his fists. "She'll call the homicide supervisor, EMS and the Commander on Duty."

"Good," I said.

"Oh, yeah," Art said. "And she'll call the crime scene unit."

"Did anyone see what happened?" Forty pairs of eyes looked at me. Several shook their heads negatively and some said, "No, ma'am."

"Nottingham? Where's Nottingham?"

Shrugged shoulders for the most part, then someone spoke up. "He's in the bathroom puking."

"Okay." I glanced around and spotted Panzarella talking to another FTO (Field Training Officer) and taking notes. "Anne, will you go tell Nottingham to suck it up and get his body front and center."

Anne nodded and left for the men's room.

We needed to get the room secure and the building perimeter secure. I needed some help. I used my cell and called Lianne Crowder, my commander. She already knew from communications what had happened.

"I've dispatched all available units to your twenty ASAP," said Lianne.

"Thanks. I don't know if this is a random sniper situation or someone after this particular cadet."

"What's her name?" Lianne asked.

"Ramona Sanchez," I said.

"I'll get someone to locate where she lives and secure her room or apartment."

For a moment the phone was silent, I thought Lianne had hung up, but then she said, "I've notified Chief Knee and Assistant Chief Jacobson. She'll handle public information and the news media." She broke the connection before I could thank her again.

There was a myriad of details that I was ill equipped to handle since I was a FNG to Homicide.

Art walked up and said, "All the exits are secure and patrol cars have blocked off the drive from our buildings out to the main street at the corner. If the sniper is still in the area, he's not getting outta here."

"Great," I said.

I walked over and looked at Sanchez's body. Her face looked serene. She lay partially on her side almost as if napping. One hand stretched towards her head and the other lay beside her torso. A large bloody area covered her chest, indicating a high caliber bullet had done great damage. Blood stained the floor. I closed my eyes and saw a young man who had been shot lying in a pool of blood. Jessie Garcia, the young man I shot last year. I took several deep breaths and opened my eyes.

This was not Garcia; it was Cadet Sanchez. I had not been the shooter. Her mortal wound had been inflicted by a high-powered rifle. Most likely one with a scope.

The Emergency Medical technicians came in and I moved away trying to get out of the way and yet not compromise the scene any more than it already had been. It was

29

obvious, however, that this room had not held the killer. The bullet had come from outside someplace. The technicians checked Ramona and in a few minutes, I saw one of them talking on a cell phone.

"You taking her to Brackenridge?" I asked. Brack was our county hospital with a top-notch trauma emergency room.

"Doctor Raines is pronouncing her here, and she'll go directly to the Medical Examiner's office."

"Okay." I made a note to find out when the autopsy would be done. I wanted to be there if possible.

The CSU technicians came and did their thing. I was too new to Homicide to give any directions, and they definitely knew their business better than I did. I knew photographs, both digital and Polaroid and videotaping would all be done. They spent time checking angles, taking measurements and blood spatters and attending to all the myriad of details that are determined to be important to a crime scene. I made a few notes for myself and a quick sketch of the girl's body.

One technician looked to be making a sketch. I watched and she was sketching the whole room to scale. How far was the body to the wall? To the windows? To the furniture? All the information was vital to the investigation and to take care of what might be needed at a trial.

I asked a technician who wielded a Polaroid camera if he would take an extra shot or two for me. When he agreed, I showed him what I wanted, he made the pictures and handed them to me when they were ready.

I stood opposite the door, looking at the line of windows along the outside wall and the first thing that caught my eyes out the window was the firemen's training tower. Could a sniper have been up there and fired on Sanchez?

Had to be. The damage done to the girl had to have been from a rifle. I couldn't see how anyone could pull out and sight a target without being somewhat hidden. A sniper could do that up in the tower.

A few moments later a CSU technician was sighting out of the window where I had been looking. Her attention confirmed my theory.

Anne walked into the room and asked if she could help in any way. "We need to get that fire tower secure," I said.

"You got it," she said, turning, and going outside.

Nottingham came out of the bathroom and stood at attention. All the cocky attitude had been scared out of him, and he was once again a young boy-man wondering what had just happened.

"You okay?" I asked.

He nodded.

"Relax, and let's sit over here out of the way. The techs need to do their thing." He nodded again. "Yes, ma'am."

We sat at some chairs just outside the doorway. Nottingham stood about five feet ten, and with broad shoulders and his cadet blues, he looked like a poster boy for APD. His dark dishwater blonde hair still had summer sun streaks, but his hazel eyes were bloodshot and red-rimmed. More reality than this kid had been ready for, I thought.

"Tell me in your own words what happened here."

"We had walked into this classroom and sat down to discuss how our role-play had gone."

"Was anyone else in here with you?" I asked.

"No, we were alone. A bunch of people were down in the rec room. I think three or four were outside in the hallway, but I'm not too sure."

"Okay, so y'all came back in here after your scenario with Anne and I?" I asked.

31

"The first thing we did after our scenario with you was go to two other role-play scenes. Then we got Cokes and snacks, and then we came back here."

"Okay." I was glad to see he was accounting for their time. It had been a good hour or so since they had acted in front of Anne and I. "So once you came in here, what happened?"

"Sanchez kept yammering on about how tough this all was and how she knew she was going to wash out. I told her she'd make it, that she just had to hang on a little while longer." Nottingham kept pulling on his left ear. He either had an earache or it was a nervous habit. Most likely the nerves.

"She worried she might wash out?" I asked.

"She said she didn't have a chance. Then she suddenly jumped up . . . I think she was crying and didn't want me to see her. She walked over there." He pointed to the windows. "She paced back and forth in the room for a time . . . maybe four or five minutes. And then I heard the sound of glass breaking and she just keeled over. She fell and blood was all over her chest."

"Where was she exactly?"

"That middle window right there. I think she looked out. Then maybe she turned back." He pulled on his ear some more. "I think she kept looking out that window, but I'm not sure. It was almost like she was looking for somebody."

Sanchez stood directly in front of the window that looked out at the fire tower. Maybe she had seen something suspicious and was just unsure of what she saw. Maybe she saw the flash of the gun or the scope for a moment, but convinced herself she was imagining things. If she saw something, why didn't she tell someone? Afraid of being laughed at, maybe?

Was somebody out after police cadets? Or was somebody out after Sanchez? Random or selective?

"Is Sanchez married?"

"No, ma'am. I think she's divorced."

"But you're not sure?"

"Pretty sure . . . well kinda sure."

"Any kids?"

"No. And I'm sure about that. We discussed my kids, and she said she didn't think she'd ever have any. That the world was so rotten she didn't want to bring any kids into such a place. She said she planned to have a hysterectomy. The big holdup in her plans is that she was Catholic, although a lapsed one, and she worried how her family would react."

"Is she from around here? The Austin area?"

"No. She's from down in the valley someplace. Some little town close to the border. McAllen, I think. Yeah, pretty sure it's McAllen."

"Okay." I made a note to check her personnel file. And someone was going to have to notify her next of kin. I made a note to call APD's Victim Services to make the notification.

"She mention anybody hassling her?"

"You mean like a stalker?"

"Yes, like that."

He hesitated.

"What?" I pressed.

"Nothing." He spent a moment thinking, pulling unconsciously on his ear. "She didn't say anybody was giving her a problem, but she seemed happier this past couple of weeks or so. I think she had a new boyfriend. She mentioned something about going to dinner with someone."

"Had she gone out or was the date upcoming?"

Nottingham didn't know.

"Did she mention this guy's name or anything about him?"

"I don't . . . I can't remember anything."

The enormity of what had just happened to Ramona Sanchez had hit him again and his face crumpled. He fought to keep control. Alpha male being tough.

"Okay, if you think of anything, call or page me." I pulled out one of my cards and wrote my electronic leash number on it. "Even if it doesn't seem important to you."

He nodded, and I walked back down the hallway.

Art Torres came over and handed me a folder. "Here's our classroom file on Sanchez."

"Thanks, Art."

Anne and Art both volunteered to assist me in questioning all the cadets. They knew these young people better than anyone. We needed to know if anyone saw anything or knew anything.

The political aspects suddenly hit me. A police cadet killed at the training Academy. I knew the assistant chiefs and probably the Police Chief himself would have to get out front and center to keep the hot heads cooled off. All we needed was a gang of vigilantes wearing police blue to go off half-cocked.

Anne and Torres left to start the questions, and I walked back into the classroom. The CSU techs were finishing up and someone asked if I was ready to release the body. I said, "Yes," and walked over for one more look at Ramona Sanchez.

I stood looking at this young woman, and thought: I didn't know you in life, Ramona Sanchez, but I have a feeling I'll know you much better. I thought about the few times I'd spoken to her, the most recent a short time ago in the non-felony car scenario.

She wasn't pretty, her face too angular, but her brown eyes had been warm and intelligent. I had thought her too timid to be a police officer. What was it I had called her in my mind? Miss Milquetoast?

In all likelihood, she would have washed out after today. "But from this point on you'll always be one of us. And I'll do my best to find out who wanted you dead, Ramona," I whispered. "I promise that much."

In Remembrance:

Cornelius L. Fahey, 35, (March 8, 1875)
Officer Fahey, a native of York, Ireland, was shot through the abdomen on an unknown block of Congress Avenue between the hours of 12 a.m. and 1 a.m. on Sunday, March 7, 1875. His assailant, a "whiskey-crazed" man named Mark Tiner, fled the scene on horseback and was captured in Hancock's pasture approximately 3½ miles north of the city. Fahey was able to identify Tiner before dying of his wounds. Officer Fahey, according to local press, "was an efficient officer, and fell while in the discharge of his duty." He is the first Austin police officer known to have died in the line of duty.

(Austin City Connection -
The Official Web site of the City of Austin)

Chapter Three

◆ ◆ ◆

Austin, Texas, the state capital, is not exactly in the center of the state, but close enough. The area is highly touted as "The Hill Country;" often it's called just Central Texas. I once wondered how to describe the hills and someone said, "Austin has hills, San Francisco has *HILLS*." But people are quite surprised to find hills and lakes and green trees, which are all due to the Lower Colorado River. I have no idea who named the river, probably someone who thought it actually was part of the Colorado River, which cuts through the Grand Canyon, although the two are not connected. The headwaters of our Colorado River are near Pecos, New Mexico.

The portion that runs through Central Texas is dammed in seven places, forming a chain of lakes: Lake Buchanan, Inks Lake, Lake L.B.J., Lake Marble Falls, Lake Travis, Lake Austin, Town Lake. They are known throughout the state as the Highland Lakes. The Hill Country with its limestone cliffs and wooded canyons is, in my opinion, the prettiest part of Texas and a major reason I enjoy living here. The other big attraction is great Tex-Mex food.

I enjoy living here, and I enjoy my job most of the time, even though I work with what could be called the dark side of humanity—crime and more specifically—homicide. The enjoyable part comes in trying to discover which bad guy it was who had done the murder. My job then becomes one of trying to stop the bad guy before he kills again, or to see him caught and imprisoned.

Today wasn't too enjoyable, however, since the victim was a young female police cadet who had been shot by a cowardly sniper. Snipers are a whole different breed of killers. Unfeeling, uncaring perpetrators and often not worried too much about being caught either. Almost as if they didn't really care one way or the other if they got caught. Yet some killers long to be caught. Writing letters to newspapers or the detectives on the case, saying: "Please stop me before I kill again." I personally hadn't run across a sniper-type killer before, but I have read some books about this particular breed written by experts on the subject.

The CSU team had gone over to the fireman's tower at the Academy, but nothing unusual had turned up. The place was full of fingerprints and the Automated Fingerprint Identification System (AFIS) was running all of them, but we were fairly sure all the prints were the firefighting cadets. No shell casings, or anything to indicate a sniper had been in the tower. No sniper worth his salt would be there without gloves. Even crooks watch television and go to movies and know how fingerprints give them away.

One of the cadet firemen told me he saw a motorcycle he didn't recognize leave from the area earlier, but he couldn't pinpoint the time. Could have been as much as two hours before the shooting.

I had reported everything to Commander Crowder, who recently had been named head of Robbery/Homicide. Lianne and I have been best friends since the Academy. Now she was my boss. After working several years in homicide, when the department head job opened up, she had applied for the position and was accepted. She was the second woman to be given that command in the Austin Police Department. Her promotion jumped over a few men who thought they should be next in line. Lianne's beauty and Raquel Welch-like figure had set off the rumor mill. Most of them swearing she'd slept her way to the top, but her case clearance rate was too high. It only took a few months for everyone to realize what a good supervisor she was, and then everyone was thrilled to be working with her and for her.

The fact that she was a newlywed did a lot to squelch the gossip. She and Kyle Raines, who had worked with me in the Repeat Offenders Unit, had gotten married three months ago. Even though he had been married to someone else when I worked with him, Kyle had been a veteran skirt-chaser for most of the time I'd known him. His romance with Lianne had begun when he'd still been married, and it had caused a few bad feelings for Lianne and me. My friendship with her had been stronger, and I couldn't stay mad at her for very long.

It turned out Kyle had fallen totally in love with Lianne and she with him. His flirting and skirt-chasing days quickly became a thing of the past. Sometimes it just takes the right woman, the right love to settle a man down. Next thing I knew Kyle had gotten a divorce, and Lianne was asking for my help in planning a wedding. She had wanted a small, but elegant wedding, and she wanted me as her matron of honor. It turned out to be exactly as she planned, and I was thrilled for both of them.

They both quickly realized Lianne was poised to move up in the department, so Kyle left APD and joined the Travis County Sheriff's Department. Neither he nor Lianne wanted any conflict between their jobs.

Lianne informed me she'd sent a couple of detectives

over to Sanchez's apartment along with a forensic team. The only thing of interest was the girl's computer. They brought that back and were going through the hard drive to find out if anything on it could be of help.

Lianne said I'd done all I could for the moment and that the only thing left undone was to discuss everything with my partner, Senior Investigator Harry Albright. He was the more experienced officer and he might have a couple of ideas.

I agreed. I was anxious to talk to Harry, but he wasn't answering his pager or his cell phone. He'd been scheduled to testify in court today and probably had not been released yet.

I decided to go see my husband and catch up with Harry later. My wristwatch read five p.m. when I walked into the two-story native limestone building, named Pecan Grove Nursing and Retirement Center, but I stopped abruptly at the nursing station. The skinny red-haired duty nurse was not anyone I had seen before. "Hi, I don't think we've met. I'm Zoe Barrow."

She ignored me.

"Nurse?"

"You have some problem?" She had a large nose and managed to look down at me with it.

"No. I was only trying to make your acquaintance. Since my husband is a patient here and I'm here almost daily, I try to meet all the nurses."

Pecan Grove was an older place, but clean and cheerful, and after Byron's parents and I had checked all over the city and within a fifty-mile radius, we had decided this was one of the best places we'd ever find. A big advantage is that it's a short twenty-minute drive for me, northward up Interstate 35 from the Austin Police Headquarters building and only a few minutes more driving from my apartment on Riverside Drive. Pecan Grove was Byron's residence, and as things stood now, it looked to be his permanent home.

The nurse pointed to the thick stack of papers on the desk. "You see those? I have to file all those in the patient charts and answer the call bells and pass out medications at eight o'clock. I don't have time to sit around and chitchat."

"Are you the only one on duty in this wing?"

"I'm the only one on duty on this floor tonight."

"Good grief. That's not right. What's happened?"

"Pecan Grove has been sold. The old staff all walked out."

"Why would they do that?" I knew some of the staff had been working at the nursing home for years. Cynthia Martin and Lucy Johnstone had been Byron's nurses the whole time he'd been here. I hated to think how he'd react to someone new.

"They didn't like the salary and benefits my company offered, so when the night shift came on at three and found out about the new company and the new rules, they all walked."

I knew it had to be something more than that to make the dedicated people I was acquainted with stage a walkout. "So, you work for the new company?"

"Yes. Been with them for five years. I came in today to get things organized and to straighten out the mess this place was in, then those incompetent ninnies walked out on me. So now if you will excuse me, I have lots and lots to do."

I turned and started down the hall to my husband's room. The woman's words and attitude told me a lot about why the nurses had walked out. But I didn't like the fact that Byron was virtually unattended. He's not capable of ringing the call bell, even if he has an emergency. He actually doesn't even know if he has an emergency.

Byron Barrow, my husband, had been on the SWAT team of the Austin Police. His team was on a mission on the night that destroyed our lives. Actually, the team's mission had been completed, everyone was all packed to go home, when a carload of gangbangers drove by and fired shots at a rival gang that lived next door. Byron still had on his Kevlar vest, but had just taken off his helmet. He took a bullet in the head. He didn't die, but the bullet's damage to his brain left him in a semi-coma.

He had remained in this state with his mind more on par with a three-month-old baby except a three-month-old baby would respond to you and Byron did not. And he'd lost mobility on one side. If you looked at him, you would think nothing was wrong. Until you looked into his eyes. No recognition. No awareness. You could tell there was nobody home inside. He could swallow and eat pureed food, but couldn't feed himself. He made sounds and noises but nothing recognizable as speech. The doctors, and there had been many, all said the effects were irreversible. No chance of recovery, they had said. His parents, Levi and Jean, and I had agreed to the painful decision to put him in a nursing home.

All the personnel were competent, as well as being warm and friendly. Byron didn't need a respirator, he breathed on his own. The nurse's aides could put him in a wheelchair for a short time as long as he was tied upright with straps, because he couldn't sit up on his own. He was incontinent and wore adult diapers. In reality, he needed what they call maintenance care, but his health insurance wouldn't pay for that. He qualified for some state aid, and my parents helped, as my cop salary couldn't manage much. Byron's father, Levi Barrow, even kicked in sometimes. I tried not to rely on either set of parents too much, although the temptation was great at times.

As I walked along the hallway, I noticed several empty beds. All of them had been occupied two days ago. I reached Byron's room and his bed was empty.

I quick-stepped, nearly jogging, back to the nurse's station. "Where is my husband?"

"And just who is your husband?"

"Byron Barrow. He's supposed to be in room 106."

"Well, I'm sure he was there at four when I did my rounds. Maybe he's down the hall talking to someone."

"Look, lady. My husband had a brain injury. He can't walk and he can't talk either. He can't get up out of his bed by himself."

"Well, then I'm quite sure I don't know. Now, if you'll excuse me I have a lot of work to do."

"Miss?" I noticed a nametag pinned to her white jacket lapel. "Miss Foster? I'm only going to say this one time." I pulled out my badge, flashed it at her, then pocketed it. "You will take a moment from all your important paperwork duties and get on the phone over there. You will call your nursing supervisor or your nursing home director. I don't care which one, but you will call right now, and you will tell them one of your patients has been snatched from his bed. Tell them it happened while you were on duty here and that I'm about two minutes from having you arrested for negligence."

She threw down the chart she held onto the counter, glared at me for about ten seconds. I already had my cuffs in my hand and was ready to haul her butt to jail when she must have finally realized I was serious. She picked up the telephone.

While she was calling her bosses, I got out my digital phone and called my partner Senior Investigator Harry Albright. I can't explain the relief I felt when he answered right away. "Harry? Byron is missing."

"What do you mean Byron is missing? From his bed? From his room? How can he be missing?"

"I don't know Harry. I don't know what . . ." I told him what I knew. "Maybe he's been placed in the wrong room or something."

"Don't think the worst, Zoe. Why don't you do a search and see if he's there somewhere in the facility? Do you want me—"

"Can you come—"

"I'll be right over," he said. "Don't panic, there's got to be a reasonable explanation."

When I hung up, Ms. Foster was looking pretty grim. "Your bosses got any answers, lady?" I asked her. "I know you don't have any."

"No, ma'am. I simply cannot imagine. But my director will be here in a half-hour."

"Let's take a little walk down this wing and see if Byron was accidentally put in another room by mistake."

Miss Foster followed me as I walked into each room. "Where are the patients in 104 and 106?"

I knew a married couple occupied those rooms, he was in 104 and she was in 106 and they had connecting doors.

"I don't know." A note of fear had crept into Nurse Foster's voice. I didn't like it any better than when she had the bad attitude. "They were all here at four o'clock," she insisted.

"And you didn't hear anything or see anything unusual?"

"No, nothing."

"Where did you get your nursing degree—Kmart?" I

muttered under my breath. We made the full search of One-East, Byron's wing. No trace of him or any of his fellow patients. We then checked the opposite corridor, One-West. No patients were missing from that side.

Only one nurse remained on duty at the central nursing station upstairs and she was also clueless. All of her patients were accounted for. I wasn't convinced she even knew how many patients she had, but took her word for it. As we walked back downstairs, I could only think that one way or the other this nurse Foster and her bosses better come up with answers pretty damn quick.

Harry arrived as we returned downstairs. He's a rock and built like a boulder, too. Six feet, four and a half inches, weighs a good two-seventy or so—I've actually never asked him for vitals. He looks in great shape. And I imagine he hits the weight room regularly, and I know he rides mountain bike trails on weekends and on days off. He and I met when a confidential informant of mine had been killed, and he was the lead detective on her case.

Harry was from the old school of policing. From the early days on the force, he always thought this job had to be too rough and demanding for a woman. However, Lianne had worked with Harry for a time, and she proved to be just what he needed to become a more enlightened male and police officer.

Harry had to be in his early fifties but only a weathered face gave that away. His light brown hair showed no gray. He sometimes made cracks about an ex-wife, but I knew his wife had died from inoperable brain cancer a few years ago. If he'd been married before then or after her death, he'd not confided in me.

Despite an age difference of ten to twelve years, Harry and I had worked so well together on that case he asked me to transfer to the Robbery/Homicide department and partner with him, which I did. I had worried early on about some of his attitudes about female officers, but he soon let me know he genuinely liked working with women investigators. "I used to worry they couldn't handle a big male subject, but found out I was wrong about that. Today's officers don't have to be big. There's a few moves anyone can use that'll handle most any size perp. Found out, too, that women are usually better at negotiating than guys are. They'll talk someone into giving up easier than I ever could."

I had to laugh. Lianne had done an excellent job educating him.

"Three patients are missing, Harry," I said after we exchanged hellos and thank you for coming. "This is unbelievable."

"Are you sure they're missing and not just moved someplace else?" Harry was dressed in black, brushed denim pants and a white and orange striped shirt with a University of Texas Longhorn logo on the pocket. He wore scuffed and worn Reeboks.

"Absolutely missing. We've checked the whole place. And two other patients are gone too. A husband and wife named Thielepape—Sam and Virginia, I think are their names."

"This just doesn't make sense," Harry's hazel eyes narrowed.

Nurse Foster gave us the key to one of the doctor's conference rooms while we waited for the Missing Persons Unit to get here. The people I wanted to see were the executives of the nursing home.

Until then, Harry and I could do a lot of speculating.

"An inside job, Harry?"

"No doubt. Only someone who worked here would know

the layout and how to remove patients without detection."

"Ambulance services? Who did they call? It couldn't be Emergency Services. Let's make some phone calls." I took out my phone. The battery was dead. "Damn, I forgot to recharge."

"That's okay, just hold-up a second anyway. How many patients are gone? And who of those were able to walk and how many needed to ride in wheelchairs?"

"Good question," I said. "I'll find out." I stood to go out to talk to Nurse What's Her Name.

"Slow down a minute, Zoe."

"What? Why?"

"This is a criminal investigation right now and needs to be treated as such—"

"This is my husband we're talking about, Harry."

"All the more reason for you to sit back and—"

"I'm not going to sit back—"

"I know that, Zoe. But we could be looking at a kidnapping and a ransom situation."

"Kidnapping." I sat back down. "I never thought—let me use your cell phone."

"Zoe. Forget calling anyone. You're not thinking straight right now. This is your husband and you're in an emotional state here."

"Damn straight, I'm in a high emotional—"

He interrupted. "Look, I only want you to sit back for a few minutes and let's see what our investigators turn up, and if you're not pleased, then you and I will see what we can turn up ourselves. Okay?"

I never got a chance to argue or agree because the other detectives arrived, and I had all the details to go over again and again. But I did agree to listen to Harry and I'd stay in the background. At least for the moment.

47

Chapter Four

◆　　◆　　◆

The funeral home looked dark except for a few yellow vapor night-lights as he cautiously tried the delivery door in back. It opened. The college boy who worked nights had done exactly what he'd been paid three hundred dollars to do.

"You just want to sit by a body?" the boy asked.

"Nothing more. Trying to prove my theory for my paper."

"And tell me again what your . . . what this is all about?"

"I want to know if the soul lingers for a while after the person has died. I think it does. I'll just sit next to this young woman's body for a little while and see if I can sense a presence. I've got permission."

The boy hesitated briefly and glanced at the computer-generated note supposedly written by her parents. "Tonight's not a good night," the boy said. "An old lady who died over in the county nursing home is due to be delivered here sometime within the hour."

"I don't need that long. Besides what happens when you receive a body? You won't need to be in the holding room, will you? Won't you just take the old lady in to be embalmed?" These small town funeral parlors, as they are called by the locals, don't play by the tight rules of the city.

"Yes, but . . ."

"All I'm asking is fifteen to twenty minutes alone with

this young woman. No one will ever know," he said. "Look, I'll give you an extra five hundred."

The kid hesitated only a moment, then held out his hand for the money, quickly pocketed it, and headed back to his chores.

A dim light lit the hallway. He could hear faint music up front, church-like funeral music, he decided. Creepy. Guess it wouldn't be too good to have a rocking soul song playing in here, even if it was late at night, he thought and looked around before he slipped into the holding room. The room held several coffins, two were occupied by corpses that had been prepared and were ready to move into individual viewing rooms come morning.

He walked up to the casket on the right and looked down at the body of the young woman who lay there. "Lonelygirl," he whispered her name as he recognized her from the sexy photo she had e-mailed him. Although she didn't look so enticing and sexy now. The slut just looked dead. He pulled off the leather gloves and slipped a pair of surgical gloves onto his hands. He looked around once more to make sure he was still totally alone. That stupid kid could come strolling back in here. He rolled "Lonelygirl" onto her side, pulling up her skirt. He smiled when he saw the butterfly tattoo on her left cheek, just like she'd been instructed. He drew the scalpel out of his pocket and quickly sliced the girl's brown skin on each side of the tattoo and peeled. Just like skinning a rabbit, he thought. He placed the skin with the intact butterfly tattoo into a Ziploc bag and stuck that into his jacket pocket and zipped it closed.

Since she'd been embalmed already, only minute traces of blood occurred and he wiped the area with a gauze pad. He removed the rubber gloves, kissed his fingertips, and placed them into the gaping wound. Then, sucking on his fingertips briefly, he glued the gauze over the spot with some paper tape, just in case there was any weeping. He rolled the body back onto her back and smoothed her dress. No one would ever know she had been disturbed. He was eternally grateful that the family had not wanted "Lonelygirl" cremated.

He walked out into the night, straddled the Yamaha, and headed north, back to Austin.

At home, and when he was clean again, inside and out, he walked into his kitchen and set the jar on the counter. He felt the warmth in his groin and the growth occurring there. He raced to the bedroom, holding the jar. He placed the jar on the bedside table, lay back, and after a few moments with his hands on his swollen gland, he masturbated. Moments later, he fell into a deep sleep.

It was near dawn when he awoke and saw the piece of skin with the tattoo on it, and was horrified. "Nasty, dirty," he said aloud. He picked up the jar and added it to the two already on the closet shelf and closed the door. He hurried to the shower and turned the water faucet to hot.

In Remembrance:

Billy Paul Speed, 22, (August 1, 1966)
Officer Billy Speed was eating lunch at a cafe near the University of Texas campus when he heard gunfire. While investigating the shooting coming from the University of Texas Tower, he was struck and killed by a rifle bullet, making him one of the first victims of Charles Whitman, the infamous tower sniper. Whitman went on that day to kill a total of 16 and to wound more than 30 others.

(Austin City Connection -
The Official Web site of the City of Austin)

Chapter Five

While Harry and I waited on the detectives to complete talking to the nursing home employees and checking for any clue to what had happened, I filled him in on the sniper shooting at the Academy. He had been testifying at a trial and had heard of the shooting but none of the details. "It had all the earmarks of a random sniper shooting, but who knows?" I said.

"So what's your take on Cadet Sanchez?" Harry rubbed the bridge of his nose with the thumb and forefinger of his left hand.

"She was a sort of quiet young woman. She might have an ex-husband around somewhere. He'll need to be looked at for sure, but I'll have to dig deeper into her life. I sure hate to think this is just some danged fool with a high-powered toy." I yawned. "I needed to get away and clear my head. I came out here to see Byron and now he's missing. How am I going to work on a homicide and still find out what's happened to my husband?"

"First off, you're not going to work on the missing patients." Before I could protest, he said, "I need you concentrating on Sanchez and what happened to her. The detectives will find Byron and the others. You know the brass isn't going to let you work on the kidnapping no matter what. The Feds may have to be called in. They have more experience and all the tools needed in kidnapping."

Harry was right. I had no business trying to find out who had taken Byron and the other patients. Harry told me his thoughts, however, after I'd calmed down. "Whoever's involved has some point to make, and they won't harm Byron and the others. It makes no sense otherwise, Zoe. They're not going to try and ask for a ransom."

"Why not? Oh, because none of us are rich."

"Right. Where's the profit in that?"

For a minute I thought he was crazy, but suddenly, I saw the sense in his words. "Harry, am I ever glad I have you around. You've got to be right."

"As usual. It was simple because you told me there's a new owner and some staff changes were being made. Maybe some of the nurses were being fired. Maybe administration plans to cut wages or benefits. I'll bet what's going on here is a strike and they're holding these patients as hostages."

It made sense to me. I was too close to the situation to think things out. "So who are they going to call and make demands to?"

"Probably the owners—"

"Maybe the newspapers and TV stations—"

"Likely," Harry said. "They already know the new owners are not going to do anything to help. Let's see what we can find out." He pulled out his cell phone. "What's the name of that news guy at channel 42 that we know?"

"So we're not going to just leave this to the other detectives and concentrate on Sanchez?"

"When you have a good idea and it feels right, you roll with it."

"I'm with you, boss." I grinned. "That TV guy's name is Tom Cole."

"Yeah, that's it. Tom Cole." Harry dialed the phone.

"Dispatch, this is Senior Investigator Albright, badge number five eight six nine, I need the phone number for . . ." he covered the mouth piece . . . "Channel 42, Zoe? KTBC?"

"No, KEYE."

"That's right, K-eye Investigates. Dispatch, I need a home phone number for KEYE TV's program manager."

While Harry got Tom Cole on the line, I went to the nurse's station and found the nursing home director was being questioned by APD detectives. They were not tippy-toeing around about it either. Three missing patients were definitely *not* acceptable.

I could feel myself wanting to join in, except I wanted to shake Nurse Foster's teeth down her throat. Before I could do anything so dumb, Harry came out.

"Tom Cole is going to do some checking with his contacts at the other TV stations and at the newspaper and see if anyone has heard anything," said Harry. "He's got our pager numbers, and he'll call if he learns anything."

"Okay, great."

"Do you have a phone number for these nurses . . . Cynthia Martin or Lucy what's-her-name?"

"Johnstone. I tried to call Cynthia just before you got here. Let me try again." He handed me his cell phone. I dialed and the phone rang and rang. "No answer. I thought she had an answering machine. She must have forgotten to turn it on."

"If she's not at home where could she be?" Harry asked.

"I don't know, and I don't know where she lives."

"I'll go ask that administrator type out there at the front desk." He walked back to the nurse's station.

I sat there and tried to get a grip on myself. Where are you my darling? I felt so helpless . . . not knowing what to do or how to do anything. Maybe I should be home in case someone like Cynthia called.

I called my home and when my answering machine answered, I punched in the code to listen to my messages and there were none.

Harry came back. "The nursing administrator gave me an address for Cynthia Martin and Lucy Johnstone. Let's pay them a little visit."

"Shouldn't we stay here?" I asked.

"For what? Byron's not here. Missing persons squad is handling things here and they don't need us interfering. They have my cell number if they need to call. I spoke with the investigator in charge and she says for us to go ahead if we have something. They'll be tied up here interviewing people."

"Okay, sounds good. I'd rather do something than just sit around." We walked outside.

"I thought so and that's what I told Stinson and her people."

"Stinson?"

"Yeah, Virginia Stinson. You met her a few minutes ago when she interviewed you."

"Oh yeah, Investigator Stinson."

"She's in charge of Missing persons. Let's go in my car, and I'll bring you back to your car later."

As much as I hated to do that, I knew I wasn't in the best of shape to drive at the moment.

Cynthia lived just off Research Boulevard and Interstate 35 North in a small duplex house between two apartment complexes. She lived in side-A, and when we checked the mailbox, Lucy Johnstone lived in side-B.

"Not the same address for Miss Johnstone as the nursing home has, but now we know where both of them are," said

Harry. He knocked loudly on the door to side-A.

No answer and I got the same results when I knocked on side-B. I tried calling Cynthia's number again. We could hear the phone ringing inside but there was no one answering and no answering machine clicked on.

"What now?" Harry asked.

"Well, I'm starving," I said. "Let's get something to eat, and we can stop by here afterwards. How 'bout Mexican?"

"Best idea you've had all day." My partner dearly hates missing meals. "Serrano's okay?" he asked. "We're not far from Lincoln Village."

He started the car while I was still hooking my seatbelt. "Okay, Harry. But we don't need to race."

"Aww, Mommy, you take all the fun outta driving."

"I know, I'm just an old meanie."

"I'm not touching that."

After we ordered, we sorted through the information I learned about Cadet Sanchez from her human resources file. "Grew up in the little town of San Juan," I said. "Parents died in a car wreck when she was sixteen. Moved to McAllen to live with three old maid aunts. Went to community college and applied to the academy fourteen weeks ago."

"Ever married?"

"Not on record. Nottingham thought she was divorced, but looks like he was mistaken."

"Did she have a boyfriend . . . maybe someone who got jealous when she broke up with him?" Harry sweetened his iced tea with six packets of sugar, putting my teeth on edge.

"All the cadets I spoke with earlier today said she was much too shy to socialize much. Not a good trait for a police officer. In fact," I said, "she was about to wash out. She couldn't hack it."

"Too bad. So she was pretty much a loner then? What about these aunts?"

"I heard from Victim Services just before I left headquarters. They talked to her Aunt Debra who said she played computer games all the time. Said she was a total computer nut. From the time she got home from work until bedtime. And all weekend, too. The girl had no social life that we can find."

"Then we must be looking at a random sniping." Harry shoveled food into his mouth about as fast as I did.

Police officers all get in the habit of eating fast. You officially have thirty minutes for a meal, but you seldom ever got that long. Even when you worked in a department where you could take the full thirty minutes or longer, you still ate fast. Old habits die hard. Medical technicians, nurses, and pilots are the only other workers I know who eat faster than everyone else.

He stopped chewing long enough to say, "A random killing is so senseless making it almost impossible to solve. Great. Just what we need."

"Makes sense to the sniper. A twisted sense to us, but perfectly clear to him or her."

"We haven't had a sniper here since Charles Whitman climbed up the UT tower," Harry said.

"Charles Whitman? Oh, the tower sniper."

Harry wiped his mouth. "In August of 1966, a troubled young man named Charles Whitman climbed the tower at the University of Texas and sniped at people all over the campus and several surrounding blocks, killing fourteen and wounding dozens before a couple of police officers were able to stop him with a bullet. I was a little kid when it happened, first grade I think, but I've read newspaper accounts and looked up Internet stories about it."

I knew that the "Tower Sniper" was the first time the whole of America became aware of a mass murderer sniper. From that time on, people realized they were not safe in their own town. They were not safe in their own neighborhood or their own community from someone who "goes berserk" and starts a killing spree.

"Yeah, I've read some about him, too. They've had TV stories through the years, too," I said.

"I think they even made a movie about the cops that shot him."

I remembered reading accounts online. The university tower is over three hundred feet high and built on a small hilltop, making it look taller than the state capitol building, although it's not. Since it wasn't too far from downtown, workers in surrounding office buildings and actually any building that was above six stories became aware from radio and television coverage of what was going on and rushed to the windows or the few television sets that were available in the office. Then bosses, secretaries, clerks, janitors, visitors, and anyone inside these buildings, all began vying for a vantage point in order to watch the scene being played out in front of their eyes. Some went up to rooftops or watched out their high-rise windows. The whole thing taking on the atmosphere of a three-ring circus.

Whitman kept firing in all directions from the tower. Wounding or killing people on campus, people going about their business on Guadalupe Street east of the tower. People coming out of restaurants or riding a bicycle down the street. It made no difference to the sniper.

First person accounts I've read told of how people couldn't understand what was going on. Someone standing next to them suddenly falling down, bleeding, falling dead or wounded. It had to have felt like a horrible nightmare.

"Man, I sure hope you're wrong, but this does sound like a random thing. Unless the shooter got the wrong person."

"Possible. But with a high-powered weapon like that, surely the shooter had a scope and knew exactly where he was aiming."

"He?" I asked.

"I mean that in the generic sense, Zoe. It could just as easily be a woman sniper."

"I'm only teasing you, Harry. I would think all sniper-types are male. All the ones I've ever heard of are anyway."

"This whole thing could get messy since a cop's been killed."

Vigilantes, I thought. When Charles Whitman was atop the University tower, a lot of men, citizens of the general public, had grabbed their guns and drove to the University campus. They had actually gathered around the tower, all trying to shoot the sniper down. Hundreds of shots were fired at the man in the tower. I don't suppose anyone protested their actions. A civilian actually climbed up with officers and assisted in the final assault on Whitman. It must have been a very surreal scene. I could see something like that happening here too but with police officers going after the sniper. I hoped we'd catch our sniper before a bunch of hothead, gung-ho cops went after him. That whole idea was scary. "You mean like cop vigilantes?"

"Exactly. It can happen in the best of families," Harry said.

We finalized the meal with coffee and split a bowl of Blue Bell Homemade Vanilla ice cream. Harry picked up the check. "I'll get this one, Zoe. You got it the last time."

My pager vibrated and I quickly scanned the message. "Uh, oh, Harry, trouble." He handed me his cell phone. I walked outside to call Commander Crowder.

"Harry," I said as he joined me in the parking lot. "We got another sniper victim out at Mansfield Dam Park . . . at Lake Travis." Harry opened his truck and grabbed his APD Police windbreaker.

"That's Travis County—"

"We've been requested to assist the sheriff's department."

"Another girl?"

"You got it."

In Remembrance:

James N. Littlepage, 67, (October 9, 1928)
Chief James Littlepage was killed during a shooting rampage in South Austin on October 9, 1928. Chief Littlepage and several officers set out from City Hall on report that a crazed man wielding a shotgun had killed two women near the 300 block of Elizabeth Street. Officers chased the man along a creek bed while Chief Littlepage drove his automobile around to head the man off. When Chief Littlepage confronted the fleeing man at the 2500 block of Wilson Street, he attempted to talk him into surrendering. The gunman shot the Chief twice in the abdomen, then ran on to a house at 1800 Newton Street, where he shot and killed a carpenter working outside the home. Eventually the gunman, barricaded in yet another house, took his own life as police closed in.

(Austin City Connection -
The Official Web site of the City of Austin)

Chapter Six

I hadn't been to Lake Travis in a couple of years, but Byron and I had spent many Sunday afternoons picnicking there when we were dating and after we married, too. It was one of our favorite places.

Lake Travis is one of the larger lakes in the chain of Highland Lakes, which were formed by damming the Colorado River. The Lower Colorado River Authority (LCRA), who manages over five hundred miles of the river, built Mansfield Dam in 1941 for flood control and water storage but, more importantly, to generate electricity. Lake Travis is west of Austin, easily accessible, and one of the most popular lakes for recreation.

The park just south of the dam, recently renovated, is operated by Travis County Parks. Facilities feature picnicking, swimming, sunbathing, camping, sailing and boating and all for an entry fee. A new addition I had heard of but not seen is an area especially set up for scuba-diving. It includes an underwater diving trail with platforms, a compass course with sunken boats, and even a sunken airplane for the divers to enter and explore.

In the days when Byron and I used to come out, there was no cost to use the park. A good thing on a cop's salary. As Harry and I drove westward, I remembered a particular Saturday when Byron and I went to Lake

Travis, planning on staying the night.

"Sure is good to get out in fresh air. Seems like I've smelled canned air for ever," Byron said.

"I know. Not even our backyard smells this clean and fresh," I answered.

"How could it with the four dogs next door?"

"That's not as bad as the lady behind us cooking heaven knows what in her barrel cooker." Byron laughed.

"It is awful, isn't it? And she keeps asking us over for dinner. I'm honestly afraid to go. Afraid of what she'll serve."

Byron laughed again. "Bar-B-Q roadkill. Armadillo, coon, squirrel . . . fresh off the Interstate."

"Taste just like chicken," I said.

"Oh, yeah. Yummy." Byron parked our car near a picnic table that was situated underneath a huge live oak tree. "Will this do, Mrs. Barrow?" he asked.

"Perfect, Mr. Barrow," I said.

We'd enjoyed swimming, sunning, eating, and since several cop friends had joined us, just enjoying good company. We had put potatoes and corn on the cob on the grill and when they were nearly done, we had grilled T-bone steaks. After sitting around a campfire and making s'mores and singing and drinking up all the beer, we had rolled out our sleeping bags, and Byron and I had cuddled together, looking at the billions of stars. During those years, the area wasn't ruined with light pollution. And so, with no moonlight to detract, we could see the faint glow of the Milky Way, and it was the best ending of a near-perfect day.

Sometime in the night, I had awakened and felt something crawling across my neck. I had reached up and felt something big, with legs. I didn't know what kind of bug, and I wasn't about to stay around and find out, either. I had screamed, waking up everybody.

"Byron, I want to go home right now."

"You mean you're going to let a lil'ole bug run you off?"

"You damn betcha I am. And what do you mean little?" It felt like something a couple of inches long. "Roll up that sleeping bag," I fairly hissed at him.

"Zoe, you're a policewoman. You can take down the biggest drug dealers in town but you're gonna let a bug destroy your camping trip? I can't believe it." Byron was obviously enjoying himself and I could hear snickers from some of the others.

"I tell you what, Buster. I've killed rattlesnakes and mice and fought screaming drunks, but I will not lay on the ground and let roaches and scorpions crawl all over me. Now I'm going back home. You can go or you can stay, it makes me no never mind. But I'm outta here."

Suddenly there was complete silence. Then a male voice said, "Scorpions?"

"Of course," I said. "They're all over the place. I killed one over there in that bathroom just about dark-thirty."

"A scorpion?" said Byron. "Those babies can sting like hell."

"I got stung by a baby one once," I said. "My hand swelled up for about three hours and it hurt like hell."

The silence was broken by the sounds of people getting up and packing up, getting ready to leave. All of them felt the same as I did, scorpion stings were not in the plans.

We left, too and Byron forever teased me about being

64

the only camper he knew who could clear a camp ground
in fifteen minutes flat.

Harry headed west on Highway 290, which connects to
Koenig Lane which is the same as Farm/Market Road 2222,
although it changes names three or four times. The evening
rush hour traffic had thinned, but traffic was fairly heavy on
a non-freeway drive. The road is full of curves and you
climb up and down hills. Too bad we didn't have a siren
and lights. Eventually, we arrived at Four Points and turned
south on Ranch Road 620. The dam is about five miles
from that intersection and the Mansfield Dam Park is on
the far south side of the dam.

If you continued south on Highway 620, you'd soon
reach the suburb of Lakeway. A new highway had been
built three or four years ago on the dam's backside, and you
can no longer drive across the dam itself. We got there in
record time, even with Harry driving like I would have, and
despite the fact that the roads the whole drive out here are
hilly and snaky.

There were numerous emergency type vehicles all
around. We found a space a short distance away, parked,
and walked over to the area lit up with portable spotlights.
The lights and people were grouped near the water's edge.
A circular patio-looking area with a metal bench was located up on the high side. There were several large boulders
that had been set in stair-step fashion from that point
leading to the water. I could see the covered body laying on
one of the lower boulders.

"Who found her?" Harry spoke to the county sheriff's
deputy who thoughtfully had kept the crime scene fairly intact by getting it encircled with crime scene tape. Thank
goodness for TV. Even the newest officers now know to

preserve the area without having to be told. Inside the area were CSU technicians from Travis County Sheriff's Department, photographing, sifting, bagging, collecting, and preserving any and all evidence.

"An Austin Citizen's Police Academy alumni group who came out here to train for Homeland Security," said the young female deputy. Her nametag read O'Neal. She was a pretty light-skinned black woman with a sprinkle of freckles across her nose, which made her look even younger. The freckles and greenish eyes and surname told of some Irish ancestor.

Not only had Travis County Sheriff's Department come out, but Lakeway Police and a couple of LCRA Rangers and two Austin patrol officers were at the scene. So many jurisdictions, but in reality the County Sheriff's Department Homicide Unit, along with their Crime Scene people, were definitely in charge here.

Today had been a balmy fall day, but now with night in full swing, a cool front had moved into our area. The north wind blew off the lake, and as I only had on a short-sleeved shirt under my APD windbreaker, I shivered. "They recruiting high schoolers now?" I asked Harry as the deputy was called back over by one of the CSU technicians.

"If she looks young to you, think how I feel—"

"Old enough to be her father?"

"More like her wizened old grandpa."

"Yeah, you are wizened, all right. Damn, it's cold." I shivered again. "Aren't you cold Harry?"

Harry shook his head and that's when I noticed he had pulled on a sweatshirt and then put on his windbreaker over that.

"Where did you get that sweatshirt? Is it mine?"

"No, it's mine. It was with my windbreaker. When I got

the jacket out of my car trunk, I grabbed it. You wanna wear it?"

I shook my head, but he took it off and gave it to me anyway. I didn't argue and thanked him as I pulled it on.

A county CSU investigator came over. "You APD Homicide?" He was in his thirties, had a shaved head and wore three rings in one ear and a diamond twinkled on the side of his nose. I'd met him once when I was working in the Repeat Offenders Unit, but didn't remember his name. His tag read Moss. "We were told to call you because of a similar case you caught recently."

"Yeah, thanks, we appreciate the call," said Harry. "What's the story here?"

"This group came out here at five—"

"Volunteers with Homeland Security?" I asked. He nodded. "But why here?" I asked.

"Because of the dam," Harry said. "All dams are considered priority because of the electric power plants."

"Yeah. Especially well-known and important dams like Hoover Dam," the technician said. "On our vacation last month we drove over Hoover, and the Homeland Security officers there stopped us and searched our motor home."

Harry looked over at Mansfield Dam, which is known as the tallest dam in Texas. "Mansfield is important to the Austin area for the electric power generated. This is the capital city, after all."

"And millions of people all down the line draw power from here," said Moss.

"Okay, so these people are somehow helping Homeland Security?" I asked.

"Someone said it was an exercise in boat patrolling or something. An all women's group. They met over there on the observation point picnic tables," Moss pointed behind where we were standing. "They brought coffee and dough-nuts as they waited for the LCRA river rangers to arrive. One lady went to the bathroom and on her way back is when she spotted something bright red that caused her to walk over for a closer look. Scared her half to death. She ran back to the table and screamed they needed to call 911.

"Fortunately for our CSU," he continued, "only one person, a retired nurse, got close enough to check that the girl wasn't breathing and then kept everyone else away until a patrol deputy got here to rope off the place."

"Best way to preserve the scene," Harry said. "Glad folks are keeping up with things by watching educational shows like *CSI*."

"I think it has made people more aware, Harry," I said. "But this group's probably had some Citizen's Police Academy training and Homeland Security training too. I've read about them in the paper. They're more knowledgeable about crime scenes than your average person, television show notwithstanding."

"Which one actually found the body?" Harry asked.

The concrete circular-bench-seating-area where the body lay was just north of the boat ramp and about fifty yards from where the women had been seated. Since the body was on the limestone rocks below the benches, it wasn't readily seen from their picnic table, especially in the dark.

The officer pointed to a small group of women huddled around a Suburban in the parking lot. "That thin one with the orange jersey and the pixie-cut hairdo," he said. "She said the only way she'd had seen this red cloth was because a car turned out of the parking lot and the car's headlights hit it. Something about it made her come closer for a better look. Think her name is Miki something-or-the-other."

I had already noted the only good light was in the parking lot, and the bulb looked dim, as if it would burn out at any time.

Deputy O'Neal walked up. "Will you two talk to them and see what you can find out? They were too upset to talk to us. My supervisor is on her way here, and she asked for your help."

We agreed. As we walked closer, we got a better look at the group. Assorted ages and sizes it looked like, seven women in all. All were dressed in slacks and wore either gray or black jackets with a Citizen's Police Academy logo on them. Some were bareheaded while others wore knit caps and gloves. They weren't going to shiver from the cold, like I was.

"Zoe, I'll take pixie-cut, if you'll talk to the group," said Harry.

I looked over at the small, but wiry woman. "Just watch out, Harry. Don't let your piggishness show, she might chew you up and spit you out."

"Oh, hell. I'll be a teddy bear. You know I'm such a good guy now since I met you."

"Ha. Well, maybe you have learned a thing or two at that."

Harry deftly cut our witness out of the pack, and they walked a few feet away.

The other women stayed huddled around the vehicle, probably to keep warm, but they all were more warmly dressed that I. "Is everyone here okay?" I asked, looking at each one. They all nodded as I caught a couple of people's eyes. "What you've seen is way out of the ordinary, but maybe some of you may have seen worse." Two of them murmured yes.

I took a small notebook out of my pocket and began

asking the obvious. "When did you get here? Did you see anything suspicious? A man or woman? A truck or a van? Is the dam a place you check on regularly?" Their answers were predictable. Nothing suspicious, no persons or vehicles were nearby. And yes, this dam was routinely checked by Homeland Security.

"Did any of you recognize the victim?"

"I . . . uh . . . I'm the only one who saw her face when I checked for a pulse. I'm a registered nurse—retired." Something about her looked familiar, but what I didn't know. "I'd like to take another look." The woman who spoke was petite, maybe mid-fifties. Her dark hair was streaked with either gray or blonde streaks; it was hard to tell in the semi-dark where we were standing. "Sondra Feemster," she said, taking off her gloves and holding out her hand.

Sondra had a strong Texas accent and a strong Texas woman handshake. I could picture her in a surgery suite or emergency room situation as being absolutely reliable and in change. She reminded me a little of my mother. "Are you sure she wasn't from your group?"

They assured me she was not.

"Each of you can look at her when CSU is ready to transport her to the morgue," I said. "To see if she can be identified."

"I don't think I want to," said the woman who looked to be the youngest. I noticed she kept struggling to hold back tears.

"You don't have to. But I'd like for you to look at a Polaroid photo, just in case, okay?"

"I guess I could do that."

"Could we each look at the photo instead of the dead girl?" one of the others said.

I wasn't sure how the Sheriff's department worked it,

but that would work for me. "I'll ask, but that's probably going to be okay."

Pixie-cut walked back to join the group and Harry motioned me over.

"Get anything?" he asked.

"One, the ex-nurse, Sondra Feemster, said the girl looks familiar, but she's unsure."

"I think maybe they all need to view her," he said.

"I agree, but how about using one of the Polaroids or a digital camera viewer? They're understandably a bit nervous about viewing the body up close and personal."

"Good idea, I'll talk to the photographer."

The CSU photographer agreed and took a Polaroid, then called to a young Austin patrol officer, Meghan Jordan, who'd come out to observe. I'd ridden patrol with Meghan when she first got out on the street. She had ultra short blond hair, green eyes, and looked like the poster child for "the girl next door." The technician handed Meghan the picture and told her to take it over to us. As Meghan walked towards us, she took a good look at the picture, and I could see her face turn white and she stumbled.

I walked quickly to Meghan. "You know her?"

Meghan stood staring off into space for a moment, then tears welled up into her eyes. "Yes, I think so. Not well. She was a class ahead of me at the academy. But I've seen her around."

"She's on the job?" Harry asked.

"But I don't know how can it be Bethany? Someone said she was on vacation all this week."

In Remembrance:

William Murray Stuart, 29, (October 16, 1933)
Sgt. William Stuart was killed in the line of duty when his motorcycle was struck by a car at the 1000 block of South Congress Avenue. Officer Stuart was attempting to pull over a speeding truck when he was struck by the car. The driver of the car was charged with negligent homicide.

James R. Cummings, 31, (December 3, 1933)
Officer James Cummings was killed in the line of duty when the motorcycle he was riding en route to an emergency call collided with a car at the intersection of 14th Street and Red River Street. Despite efforts by Cummings' partner and the occupants of the car to carry Officer Cummings to nearby Brackenridge Hospital, he died almost instantly from his wounds. Officer Cummings was the second motorcycle officer to be killed in the line of duty in less than two months.

(Austin City Connection -
The Official Web site of the City of Austin)

Chapter Seven

"Let me see," said the ex-nurse, wrinkling her forehead. She looked at the photo more closely. "Yes, that's why she looked familiar to me. I'm sure I've seen her out at the Academy. Probably at one of the functions where we served refreshments to the cadets or something. Maybe even graduation."

"Yes, I remember now, too," said Miki something-or-the-other. "I think she graduated in the class last fall. Metford? . . . no . . . Maynard?" She kept snapping her fingers. "Yeah. Oh, yeah. It was Mayfield. I went to school with a Terry Mayfield and I wondered if she was related. Turns out this girl was adopted and no relation to my friend . . . Bethany Mayfield. She's from New Mexico. But that's all I remember."

"So that makes three people who thinks it's Bethany Mayfield," I told Harry. "Semi-official identification."

"We'll be able to get her records and make notification now that we know who she is," Harry said.

The CSU technician, Moss, walked over. "Albright? Can y'all come over here for a moment?"

"Sure thing," Harry said as he turned back to pixie-cut and the nurse. "If you two don't mind, I'd like you to go to headquarters and make a formal statement of what you've told us." He motioned to Meghan. "Officer Jordan? Will you escort these women downtown and then bring them back to their cars?"

Meghan said, "Sure, no problem."

Pixie-cut looked around. "What about the others?"

I said, "None of them saw much. We'll need everyone's name and address, and then they can go on home."

Meghan said they had already gotten all that information from the others.

"Okay," Miki something looked a bit dismayed. "I didn't bring my car. I rode out with Sara." She motioned to the youngest woman.

"That's okay, I'll take you home." Sondra patted the other woman's shoulder then looked at me. Harry had already turned and was walking over to the location of the body. "Is it okay if we take my car downtown, this officer can lead or follow us and—"

"That's fine," I told her. "We'll make it easy on everybody."

Officer Jordan and the two women turned to leave, and I walked over to join Harry. The medical examiner tech was explaining that the victim had been shot with a high-powered rifle. Duh, I had figured that one out.

"Probably a top of the line, Mauser or Remington. Top of the line scope, too."

"Same as Ramona Sanchez," I said. "Did we get ballistics on that yet, Harry?"

"Just that it was a .30 caliber. A bullet they dug out of the floor had ricocheted and was too mangled to be much good."

"And CSU didn't find any casings in the tower either. Anything out here?"

"Nope," said the technician. "It looks like she was pacing around like she was supposed to meet someone and was waiting for them."

"And whoever it was that met her, shot her?" I asked. "Maybe a jealous boyfriend followed her out here. She met another guy and the boyfriend shot her."

"I think it's most likely someone was already waiting here for her," said Harry. "If she heard a car approaching, wouldn't she go towards it?"

"Sure," the tech and I both answered.

"But you did say it was a rif—" I said. "Then why use a rifle? A rifle is so impersonal. Why not use a handgun if you wanted to kill someone specifically."

"Maybe the killer didn't know her," said Harry. "This can still be a random sniper. Someone who has a hard-on for female officers."

"But he must have known her well enough to lure her out here," said Moss.

"None of this makes good sense," I said. "And I'm wondering how a new cadet like Ramona Sanchez and this policewoman named Mayfield could be connected. Had they worked together? Did they even know each other?"

"It makes sense to the killer." Harry's voice was husky. "We've just got to get into his head and figure out what he's thinking."

The CSU technician Moss said, "A rifle indicates the killer was located—" Harry and I both turned and began scanning the area.

"There's three or four likely places." Harry pointed. "Especially from the dam."

I started to move towards the dam.

"Wait up, Zoe. It's too dark now and if we go tramping around over there, we'll mess up any evidence that's there." He looked at his watch. "Let's wait until we can see."

"But dammit . . ." I didn't like waiting around but Harry had a point.

"Besides," said Harry, "I think the dam is too far away now that I look over there."

Moss, the technician, said, "It probably is too far away, and you're right, we can't see a dang thing out here. We don't have all those high-powered lights like they have on TV. We'll definitely need daylight to do a good job. We'll get a deputy to stay out here to keep the area secure."

"LCRA Rangers can block it off and keep people out of the park," said Harry.

"Okay, I guess," I said. "So what do we do until daylight?"

"Let's go to headquarters and get the ID nailed down on the victim, and someone will have to give Travis County's Victim Services the information to notify the next of kin. We need to know if she had family in the Austin area. Find out where she lives, if she has a boyfriend? A room mate?" Harry's brain was clicking on all cylinders now. "Find out her work schedule. That patrol officer, Jordan, said she thought the gal was on vacation . . . we need to check that out."

"Okay, Harry. Don't mind me." As a FNG homicide detective, I'd defer to Harry's expertise.

"Look, kiddo. After everything you've been through tonight . . . you're entitled to a mental fart or two."

"You do have a way with words, Harry."

"Yeah, just call me the silver-tongued devil." We headed back to his Crown Vic and while I made a few cell phone calls hoping to get more information on our victim, he concentrated on driving.

I had not forgotten that my husband and some of his fellow patients were missing from Pecan Grove, but I honestly wasn't as worried as before because I felt sure Cynthia Martin knew where they were, maybe was with them, and would take care of everyone properly, especially Byron. He was her special patient.

Just as we reached Austin Police headquarters on Eighth Street, my cell phone rang. We pulled into a parking space and answered. It was Cynthia. "I need to talk to you."

My cell phone went dead. "Battery's dead again," I told Harry. "But that was Byron's nurse."

"Use my phone," Harry said.

"I don't have her number. It was on my phone but with the battery dead I can't see the read-out." I shook my head trying to think straight. "I guess I could go back to her place."

"Go," said Harry. "Go out there and see what you can find out. Call me if there's anything I need to know."

"My car is out at Pecan Grove," I said.

Harry quickly drove me back to my car and said he'd head back to headquarters and meet up with me later.

I drove back down Interstate 35 and exited on Highway 183, turned left under the interstate and then right. A short block north took me to the duplex and I parked across the street. The house was a small frame with siding halfway up. It was painted a battleship gray. Someone had tried to relieve the monotony by painting the windows and door frames a dark hunter green. The Bermuda grass was trying hard, but the weeds looked as if they'd win. One Mimosa tree was on the A side and a small evergreen stood at the corner of the house on the B side. A row of short yellow and green shrubs of undetermined origins crouched under the windows on either side of the door. I imagine Cynthia and Lucy rented the duplex and the owner did as little as possible to keep the place up.

I couldn't see any lights shining from either side, which puzzled me. If Cynthia and Lucy were there with Byron and two other patients, why were they all in the dark? I could feel a knot forming in the middle of my stomach as I reached the front entryway and door. I rang the bell on Cynthia's side. Side-A. No answer. There was no response from Lucy's side-B either.

I walked around to the back and the house was as dark as the inside of an undeveloped limestone cave. Not only was I puzzled, I was frustrated and beginning to be upset. Where were they and what the hell did these nurses think they were doing?

I knocked on the doors of a couple of houses across the street. Only one person answered, and he swore he hadn't seen anything. By the sound of the televised football game in the background and the smell of beer that radiated from him, I felt sure he was being truthful.

The only other neighbors were in the apartment complexes on either side, and I didn't have the manpower to canvass those. Actually, the missing person's squad could probably take care of that. Since my cell phone battery was dead, I drove to the corner gas station/convenience store and when the outside pay phones proved to be out of order, I persuaded the store clerk to allow me to use the store's phone. English wasn't first or probably not even his third language, but the police ID badge means the same in any language. He handed me the telephone.

I reached Harry on his cell. "I'll call over to missing persons's and talk to Detective Stinson," he said. "See what progress they've made."

"Do you think we should—" I began.

"We shouldn't do anything at all. Let Missing Persons handle it. You come on back to headquarters."

"Harry, I need to do—"

"What? You don't know where they are. What direction

they took? Anything?" His voice got softer. "You know those nurses aren't going to hurt their patients. Besides if Cynthia can't reach you on your cell, most likely she'll try to reach you through this number."

"You're right, Harry. You must think I'm a total flake or nutcase."

"No. I just know you're upset. When you get here, we'll try to come up with a plan. We'll find Byron. And I'm confident Cynthia and Lucy will keep him safe."

"See you in a few." I thanked the flustered young store clerk and hurried out to my car.

As I drove, several possibilities came to mind about what Cynthia and Lucy had planned, but then I realized they probably had no plan. They most likely had acted totally on impulse when they left Pecan Grove Nursing Home.

Impulse is usually a principle that Byron and I often used to go off for a weekend. It wasn't that often we could get the same weekend off-duty so when we did manage it, we'd throw a tent and some camping gear into the back of his pickup and head for the hill country. We'd leave town as quickly as possible so we wouldn't be available by phone if someone called. We wouldn't even buy groceries in town, we'd stop at an HEB grocery or a Wal-Mart someplace and get what we needed.

One of our favorite places to camp was Inks Lake State Park. It's about an eighty-mile drive, west of Austin. It's also right on the lake. Many campsites are near the lake's edge. Inks Lake is one of the Highland Lakes chain. The park itself is large and can be too crowded on holiday weekends or in late spring. But most weekends in the winter in central Texas are mild enough for camping if you have a good tent and sleeping bag.

We would take our bicycles and Byron would take

fishing gear. I'd take my camera, and I'd take hundreds of photos of birds like blue herons, red-tailed hawks or eagles. And of course, all the wild life: white tail deer, skunks, possums, raccoons, squirrels, and rabbit. I loved watching deer and Inks Lake State Park is home to herds and herds . . . probably several hundred deer. The grounds are cleared around the trees in the camping areas, and the deer come up and munch the grass and then bed down . . . often only ten feet from your tent. You really feel close to nature here, and Byron and I both loved that feeling.

Now if coyotes or bears did this, then I'd be worried, but I didn't mind sleeping near Bambi and his momma.

Besides missing the companionship of my husband on a daily basis, I also missed him for things like camping trips that I don't take anymore. Some of my officer pals go camping in west Texas to Balmoral State Park and are into scuba-diving. They have asked me to go, but somehow I'd feel like I'd be betraying Byron if I went on a camping trip and had fun. Silly, I know, but still the guilt is there.

I pulled into a parking spot right alongside headquarters and knew it was only because of the late hour that I was so lucky. I was tired and all I wanted was to get in, get out, and head home.

As I walked inside our office, I found Harry talking on the phone. He waved me to a chair. "What's up, Harry?"

"We've got some new information on our shooter, Zoe. We need to go down to the ME's office and discuss it with Doctor Voss."

"Tonight?"

"I know what time it is, but this is going to blow your mind, Zoe. This sniper is a junkyard dog."

In Remembrance:

Elkins P. Morrison, 29, (February 2, 1936)
Officer Elkins Morrison was killed in the line of duty when he was struck by a car at the 300 block of Congress Avenue. Officer Morrison was on detective duty when he was struck crossing the street. Darkness, fog and rain were blamed for poor visibility leading to the accident.

Walter Lee Tucker, 26, (October 14, 1948)
Officer Walter Tucker was killed in the line of duty when the motorcycle he was riding collided with a car at the intersection of Monroe and South Congress Avenue. Tucker, a two-year veteran, was on traffic patrol when the collision occurred.
(Austin City Connection -
The Official Web site of the City of Austin)

Chapter Eight

◆ ◆ ◆

Harry Albright had been a cop for so many years that few things ever shocked him. "Been there, done that, and bought the T-shirt," he'd say. But I'd worked with Harry long enough to know our sniper got to him in some inexplicable way. His voice shook with emotion when he said we absolutely had to go to the coroner's office, and I thought I detected a quiver. It just wasn't like him to be this upset.

What had shaken this tough old Homicide dick? I wondered as we headed down to the police garage. I asked him what was wrong. He just said we needed to talk to Doctor Voss. "Pointless for me to discuss it," he did say after I asked again.

I headed to his unmarked sedan. I was just too dammed tired to argue about who would drive or to even worry about it. For once Harry actually drove a normal rate of speed. Of course, at this time of the evening, there was virtually no traffic except for a few cars on Sixth Street.

A tiny sliver of moon showed in the eastern sky. It was hard to keep my mind on everything that had occurred in the past few hours. I knew I needed sleep before I could absorb it and make good sense out of it all. Too much information and too little time. My body walking around with the brain barely clicking on one cylinder.

I'd read an article recently that said when you kept going

for long hours without sleep, your body becomes as sluggish as if you were drunk. You might not blow a .08 on the Breathalyzer, but your reaction time was certainly in that category. I could relate. I knew my reaction time right now was about the speed of molasses in winter.

We cruised past the newest downtown building, the Frost bank tower with its weird spires, but when all lit up at night, gave off a silvery glow. Austin's downtown buildings are outlined in Christmas lights that now stay lit all year. Somehow it makes the area warmer and friendlier. Harry didn't talk, and when I tried to question him, he only grunted. Obviously, he would show and not tell me what was going on.

Next we drove past the pink granite of the Capitol building and the white, gothic-style Governor's Mansion. Both all lit up and sending out welcoming glows. Sleep well, Governor and First Lady, your Austin Police Department is on duty taking care of your city. Was I sounding a bit sarcastic? Probably, but sleep deprivation always did strange things to me.

We got parked and hurried into a side entrance of the building that housed the ME's office. The hallway's blue-white fluorescent lights were garish and institutional. But I wouldn't expect candles in a city morgue, just something a bit more subdued.

Once inside I took a good look at Harry. "You know, you've put a bit of a scare in me . . . I don't think I've ever known you to be so uncommunicative."

He gave me a weak grin and said, "Let's go back here and talk to Doc Voss."

Harry pushed open the door leading to Voss's office and we walked in. "Hey Doc, have you met my partner, Zoe Barrow?"

"Don't believe so," the doctor said. "But she does look somewhat familiar. Did you take any classes out at UT?" Doctor Voss was a legend around the police department, as well as at the University of Texas. He had taught forensic classes twice a week several years ago. He was thin with an extremely large Adam's apple, lank dark hair had been combed over to partially cover a balding head. His looks, however, had nothing to do with the man's incredible intelligence.

"I took a couple of your classes at UT, doctor. How are you?"

"Quite well, thank you."

"Do we have a problem here or what?" I asked. Both men were driving me crazy; Harry with his attitude and the doctor with his polite chatter. "Please, will one of you tell me what's wrong?"

"I want to show you something about your latest victim, and then I'll have something important to tell you afterwards."

Now they both had me a bit worried. Was the latest victim some movie starlet we somehow failed to recognize? Some relative of the APD brass? Was this case going to rise up and bite me in the behind or what?

Doc escorted me through the door leading to the examination room. If I thought the outside looked stark, this room went beyond. Everything all white and stainless steel and glaring white lights, cold and stark. Just what was needed for this room, I imagined. I heard an intake of breath behind me and realized Harry had followed along. The latest sniper victim was lying on the stainless steel table draped with a white sheet, with only her face showing. Doc Voss walked up to the table and lifted the sheet on the woman's left side, rolled her and motioned me closer.

He showed me her left buttocks. At first I wasn't aware of what I was looking at, and then I realized part of her skin had been stripped away. A fairly large area . . . perhaps three by five inches of skin. What was left there was bloody; a yucky, oozing spot with some yellowish stuff surrounding it. The wound was ragged, looking somewhat torn, almost as if a dog had chewed on it.

I swallowed hard so as to not throw up. It would never do to throw up in Harry's presence. "Oh my God. What happened here?"

"My thoughts exactly," said Doc. He took a surgical-looking instrument from a nearby steel table that looked like a TV tray, and pressed it against the woman's flesh. "At first, I thought maybe some animal had taken a chunk out of her postmortem. Officer Mayfield was found out at Mansfield Dam Park, right?"

We both nodded.

"Actually, this *was* done postmortem but not by an animal. At least not a four-legged one." Doctor Voss' voice dropped into instructor mode. "Took a minute, then I remembered something about your first sniper victim . . . police cadet . . . Sanchez? She had a blue butterfly tattoo on her left buttocks. Almost the exact location of this wound on Miss Mayfield."

The doctor cleared his throat. "So I called the funeral home where we released the body to, Goddard's Funeral Parlor. It's in a small town down in the valley, and the director there told me, yes, Sanchez had a butterfly tattoo on her left buttocks, he remembered seeing it when they dressed her. Her funeral service is tomorrow."

Doc paused and took a deep breath. "I asked him if he would go and check her tattoo and give me some exact dimensions on it and get back to me. He called me back about a half-hour later and told me someone had broken into their embalming room and peeled Miss Sanchez's hide . . . stripping off the butterfly tattoo. Just like this one."

"So this means what? Our sniper is killing women with a high-powered riffle and then getting to their bodies and stripping off their tattoo?" I asked.

"Yes. And I'm not sure what he's using to remove the skin . . . a filleting knife maybe? Here and here, but over here . . . uh, this. . . ." Doc pointed to some indentations on the smooth skin. "These marks up here look a lot like teeth marks and a hickey. Like he sucked on it and then bit the spot before he began stripping it off."

"Oh, yuck." My gag reflex kicked in, and I hurried out of the exam room and found a bathroom. I didn't upchuck, but I came mighty close to it.

When I came out, Harry didn't even make a crack. He just asked if I was okay. "I'm fine, but damn and double damn, Harry. I thought psychos like this only hung out in big cities like New York or Chicago or L.A."

"Welcome to the real world, kiddo. It ain't never been pretty here in my town, but it looks like it's only going to get uglier. One good thing, Doc says he's got good DNA from the wound. If and when we get a suspect, we'll be able to tie him to the mutilation."

We thanked Doc for his heads-up investigative work and asked him to keep the information quiet. "We don't need the press knowing all the details," Harry said as he shook hands with Doc. "They're going to be digging for info as soon as they realize both women were killed by the same type of rifle. Will you call and clue in that funeral director down in the valley?"

"I already asked him to keep it quiet for the obvious reasons," said Doc.

"Okay," said Harry. "But call him back and tell him we'd like to send down a CSU team to gather any DNA or print evidence."

"Okay, but the funeral is tomorrow at two p.m."

"We'll get a team down there tonight and if we're lucky they'll be finished in time for the services."

"You think the police department down there will let our forensic team in to do anything?" Doc asked.

"I'd better call the Commander and see if she can grease the wheels," said Harry. He pulled out his cell phone and started punching numbers.

"It just so happens I know the coroner down there," said Doc Voss.

"Well, you old curmudgeon, why didn't you say so to begin with?" Harry said.

"Because I just now remembered who it was. Sorry, Harry," said Voss.

"Yeah, yeah. Okay, go ahead and see what you can get going. I still need to talk to Commander Crowder and let her work it from that angle." Harry's voice was all business now. "We'll need all the help we can get to get this done before releasing the body for the funeral."

Harry and I walked outside. He asked about Byron, and I clued him in on the empty duplex. We got into his car and started back to headquarters.

"I still think you don't really have anything to worry about."

"Harry?" I said. "I'm going to go home . . ."

"Let me report in to Lianne, but you and I need to have some discussion on this new development tonight. Want some pie or dessert?"

"No, Harry. I've lost my appetite."

"How about coffee?" Harry drove at a much faster

driving speed than he had on our trip over, but there wasn't any traffic for me to worry about.

I said okay, then Harry threw a bombshell I had not seen coming. "Are you seeing Jason Foxx?"

"Hello? When did my social life become your business?"

"I was just asking a simple question, don't get your panties in a twist."

"I haven't seen or heard from Jason in a couple of months. You know I'm not interested in dating anyone, and that includes Jason Foxx."

"I know you're not wanting to date anyone . . . I just thought . . . oh hell, it ain't none of my business anyway," Harry said.

He spotted my car and drove up beside it, double-parking.

"Okay, now that we've got my social life straight. . . ." I reached for the handle and opened the car door. "Is Denny's okay? Just coffee if we have to talk, a little caffeine . . . otherwise I'll nod off."

"I'll race you over."

Harry beat me by a good five minutes, and he'd already gotten us a table. "I ordered coffee for us both and a slice of pie for me. Coffee was all you wanted, right?"

"That's fine. So what did Lianne say?"

"She pushed it up to HQ. Let them make the call, but I think a CSU team will head down there tonight and see if there's anything we can use."

"Did Doc call down and talk to his friend?" I asked.

"Yes, everything's lined up."

Our coffee came and as Harry ate his lemon pie, he made small talk about sports, trying to put a sense of normal back into our lives. We ordered more coffee, and the talk once again turned to our case.

"Okay, Zoe. What have we got here besides the bizarre?"

"Two female officers shot with a high-powered rifle . . . indicating a sniper-type killing," I said.

"But these victims were not picked at random?"

"I don't think so. Both have several commonalities. Both were policewomen . . . one a cadet. . . . both were Mexican-American," I said.

"Which indicates what?" asked Harry.

"Somebody's got a hard-on against policewomen and especially Mexican-American women. These women probably were not chosen randomly," I said. "He probably knew both women, so we need to dig more into their backgrounds."

"Absolutely. First thing in the morning, I want you to do as deep a background as you possibly can."

"Not tonight?" I managed to ask.

"No, go home and get some rest. We can't think straight when we're this tired. We'll get a good start first thing in the morning."

"I knew you weren't an unfeeling person. You've just been running on caffeine so long you've forgotten how tired we younger folks can get," I said.

"You've just got to learn how to pace yourself."

"I know, Harry. Like running a marathon. I'm afraid you'll always be able to work rings around me and you're ten years older."

"Comes from eating my Wheaties every morning."

"Yeah, right." I stood and grabbed our check and hurried to the cashier.

As I drove home, I realized how exhausted I was. I parked, walked up to, and opened my apartment door. My cats, Melody and Lyric, greeted me as if I'd been gone a week. Dancing around my feet, both vying for immediate attention. "I know, guys. But if you knew how to open the cat food, would you even care?"

"Miooow," said Lyric, the vocal one. Melody, usually the quiet, shy one, gave out some soft little, "Mewt, mewts" which sounded almost like a baby goat. I poured food in their bowls and gave them fresh water. "Give me a little time for me, then I'll pay you more attention," I told them, but they ignored me, preferring to eat.

I quickly undressed and took a warm bubble bath, dozing in the tub. Wrapped in a long terry robe, I settled down with Melody on my lap and Lyric beside me while I drank a glass of Merlot. Lyric has a tendency to drool on you when you hold him, and since I'd already had my bath and was dressed for bed, I didn't need a bath in cat saliva. When I got up to take my glass to the kitchen, I noticed the message light on my answering machine was blinking. One message was from Jason Foxx. "Haven't heard from you in a coon's age, Zoe," he said. "You mad?"

No, I wasn't mad, I thought. I just wasn't sure how I felt about the guy. I wasn't sure if I could be friends with him or if I should stay away from him. I think I'd like to be his friend. Can a man and a woman ever be just friends? Maybe not, if there's sexual tension between them.

Jason had been a cop in Houston but had to take a medical leave after being shot. I had the impression his recovery emotionally had been slow and rocky. He told me his marriage broke up over it, but he really didn't like to talk about what had happened.

He and I had worked well together . . . even obtaining that cop-think where we almost finished each other's sentences. He'd been recommended as a private investigator by a lawyer friend, and I sent him to help a friend of my father-in-law. Later, Jason actually wound up helping me catch the guy who had killed my confidential informant, Tami, a few months back.

Jason and I had had dinner a couple of times. He looked a little like that Brad Whitford guy, the actor from *The West Wing*, except Jason had carroty-red hair. I've had an aversion to red-haired guys ever since being dumped in the third grade by red-headed Lanny Wiseman. However, things about Jason excited me. Stirred emotions that I wasn't sure I wanted stirred. I didn't need exciting men in my life. I'm still a married woman.

This is not a place I'd wish to be in, nor would I wish it on anyone else either. A type of limbo; my husband alive but not with me emotionally or mentally. And I honestly still loved my husband. I had promised to love him in sickness and in health. I kept holding on to the hope there would be some improvement in Byron's condition, despite what the doctors had told us.

"I'll call you back tomorrow, Jason. I'm too tired tonight," I said aloud to the cats. They didn't answer.

One message was from Harry. He must have called while I was in the shower. "I hope you've already gone to bed. I need you bright and bushy-tailed first thing in the morning. And although I didn't tell you so, I'm glad you aren't seeing Jason. The guy is rude and obnoxious . . ."

I pushed the off button, laughing at Harry. He really liked Jason, and I think he thought by using reverse psychology on me, he would play matchmaker. Harry thought I should go out sometime and have some fun. Everyone else who knew me thought so, too, including Byron's parents, Levi and Jean Barrow.

No one wanted me to write Byron off, but as my mother said, "Zoe, you need to have a life besides your work."

I told her, I had a life. "I go places with friends, movies, ball games, lunch and shopping."

"That's not what I mean," my mother said.

"I know what you mean, mother, but there are many people in this world who face this same limbo I'm in and they survive." Maybe I will go out on a "date" one of these days, I thought. But with Jason Foxx? My emotions about him scared me a little too much.

I fell into bed, and the cats snuggled against my legs and feet, and in only moments, I didn't think about anything or anyone else.

In Remembrance:

Donald Eugene Carpenter, 28, (January 30, 1964)
Officer Donald Carpenter was killed at the site of a burglary in progress. As officers surrounded the business, a suspect inside shouted that he was coming out, but instead opened fire. Officer Carpenter was just exiting his patrol car when he was struck by gunfire from inside the building. Another officer already on the scene was seriously wounded. Officer Carpenter, shot in the head, died two days later.
(Austin City Connection -
The Official Web site of the City of Austin)

Chapter Nine

◆　◆　◆

Bright and early the next morning, I drove down Riverside Drive to Interstate 35, listening to a local talk/news radio station. When they started discussing a squabble going on between the mayor and the city council, I switched over to Sammy and Bob at KVET, a super popular country station. Those two could put smiles on your face no matter what mood you happened to be in. Today they were talking about a concert by Dolly Parton the evening before. Their discussion was how good she looked and sounded. But one of them (I can never tell which one is Sam and which one is Bob) complained that she talked too much instead of singing, while the other enjoyed all the small talk. Then they spent a good five minutes discussing Dolly's healthy chest. Yet they were never tacky about it, only funny.

At eight thirty, the traffic was unusually light on Riverside Drive where my apartment is located, but increasingly got heavier as I neared Interstate 35 and headed north.

I could tell the day was shaping up to be warm, but the humidity was low, and that would keep the higher temperatures more pleasant. Austin's skyline looked bright and shiny in the morning sun, hiding its darker side of the evening, like most cities. Something about the bright newness of the city after the horrors of the night before helped renew my spirits.

quarters needed better protection. A counter that looks a lot like a bank counter but with glass above it. That new part reminds me of a movie theater ticket booth.

Now the lobby is small and somewhat ugly looking in my opinion. But the glass is probably bulletproof and the counter lead-lined, and the officers behind it are well protected and all the officers upstairs have more protection.

Detective Cherokee Hack was a cute dark haired thirty-something officer who I recalled had attended some of my classes out at the academy. Cherokee is only a tiny part Native American, but enjoys wearing braids and feathers on her off days. She is cheerful and likable, and also is extremely bright and computer literate. These attributes are most helpful in her position as supervisor of the reception area. She must deal with every segment of the public, from the extremely rich to the homeless, from the saints to the sinners, from the good and the evil, any and all persons who walk into Austin Police headquarters.

I usually park in back in the garage and walk in the back door, but today I knew I'd be going back out again within a few minutes and so had parked in front.

Cherokee turned to look at me, as did two soccer-mom-type women. "Hey, Zoe? You working on that homicide from out there at the dam?"

"Yes." I hesitated, hoping these were not family members. The sun was bright outside and my eyes had not adjusted yet.

"These women may have some information for you." She smiled a big smile. "I tried to reach Harry, but he's not answering the phone up there." She rolled her eyes upward towards the homicide department.

"Knowing Harry, he's in the coffee room, and he hates

to answer the phone before he's had his morning quota of caffeine," I said.

As I walked over closer, I recognized the two women from the Homeland Security group last night. "Hello. I'm Zoe Barrow. We met last night." I held out my hand.

One was our pixie-cut female witness who discovered the body whose name I never got for sure . . . Miki something-or-the-other. The other lady was Sondra Feemster, the retired nurse. They both nodded and shook hands. Sondra introduced me to the pixie-cut lady as Miki Bellah. "Miki here needs to speak to you or that nice Sergeant Albright, who was working with you last night," said Sondra.

"Why don't we go upstairs where we can sit down and be more comfortable and where Sergeant Albright can join us?" They agreed.

Cherokee handed me two visitor passes, and we headed back to the elevators. I pushed my ID card into the slot and pushed the button for the third floor. You couldn't get past the second floor without the proper identification. That was one of the safety measures taken long before 9/11. I used to think it had been designed to keep the riffraff away from the top brass, but soon realized it kept all of us safe from anyone intent on harming the officers who worked in this building. You certainly wouldn't want someone who swore to kill you while on trial to come after you when he got paroled four years later.

When we reached Homicide, I asked the two women to wait in one of the interrogation rooms and went to get coffee for them and for myself and to look for Harry.

Predictably, I found him in the coffee room. He looked much too chipper for this time of the morning and our late night hours, but Harry likes mornings and I hate 'em.

"What's up, Zoe?" he asked, as I reached for my cup and

poured it full. I added both cream and sugar and watched Harry shudder as I did so. He thinks the way I drink coffee is for wimps and kids. My favorite way to drink it is with mocha flavoring or with Kahlúa. Not exactly my favorite drink, but the caffeine does help me wake up, and so I drink it.

"Two of the women from the sniper scene last night," I said. "Not sure, but I think they have more info for us. It's Nurse Sondra Feemster and pixie-cut, Miki Bellah."

"Great. We need a break."

I placed the mugs of coffee for the women on a small tray, added packets of creamer, sugar and Splenda, a no-cal sweetener. I added my own cup, and the two of us headed back to where the ladies waited.

Both women were seated in the stark room that had white walls that looked like they needed paint when George Bush, Senior was president. Both women had their hands folded in front of them on the metal utility table, looking like a couple of kids waiting on the school principal to come in and give them demerits.

As soon as we walked in, Nurse Sondra Feemster spoke up. "I told Miki she absolutely had to tell you what she saw, even if it's not important." Sondra looked to be someone that others could count on in any situation. I could picture her keeping a bunch of prima donna doctors in line. It was just an air of confidence in her demeanor. She had short champagne-colored hair with darker streaks in it, and blue/grey eyes. A pair of wire-rimmed glasses hung on a gold-colored chain around her neck.

"I . . . uh . . . it was more something odd," Miki said. "I totally forgot about it." Miki Bellah's auburn hair, cut in that pixie style, over-emphasized her dark brown eyes. Maybe that was the point, as she did have large, luminous eyes, intelligent, with a hint of mischief. She was small boned but well muscled, and a few freckles showed up on her tanned skin.

"Why don't you tell us what you remember and let us decide. Any piece of information could be the exact puzzle piece we might need," I said. "Of course it may not, and, in which case, we give you a gold star for effort." I tried for a light touch in order not to spook her too much.

Harry said, "Zoe's right. Something that sticks in your mind as an oddity could be exactly it." Harry was using his fatherly, concerned voice.

"Go ahead, Miki. They're not going to think you're strange or anything like that," Sondra prodded gently.

"Well," Miki began. "I always get out to the dam earlier than anyone else. I have a horror of being late to anything . . . an appointment with the doctor, a party or whatever." She fiddled with her bangs that were too long. "What I usually do is bring some needlework or something to occupy my time while I'm waiting."

Neither Harry nor I spoke, giving her a chance to collect her thoughts and continue.

"So I'm sitting there in my car knitting and I heard a motorcycle. It was really loud, a deep roar. But when I looked up it was over close to that little camper store building. I think it was someone who was just riding through the park. I don't see how that person had anything to do with killing, do you?" Miki asked.

I saw Harry's glance and recognized it. This could be the break we needed. "Maybe, maybe not," I said.

"This happened probably an hour earlier, before I saw the body, and that camper store is just such a long way from where the body was found, all the way over on the other side of the picnic area actually," Miki said.

"What kind of motorcycle was it?" Harry wanted to know.

"A big, black one. I don't know anything about motorcycles," Miki said.

"Could it have been a Harley?" Harry asked.

"Like a Harley-Davidson," I prodded, thinking maybe she needed to hear the full name.

Sondra patted Miki's arm. "Just think back."

Miki closed her eyes for a few seconds, then opened them. "I don't know. That's the only kind I think I've ever heard the name of, but I don't know if that was a Harley or not. It was big and black and evil-looking."

"Evil-looking?" I asked. "In what way was it evil?"

"I can't explain it, but it looked evil," she had a strange expression on her face. "That's partly why I hesitated to come in . . . I thought you'd laugh at me."

"No one is going to laugh at you, Miki," I said. "Sometimes we women have intuition about things and most of the time we can't explain it." She was nodding as I spoke. "It's just a feeling we have and there's no explanation."

"That's exactly how I feel," Miki said.

"If we showed you a map of the park, do you think you could point out exactly where you saw the motorcycle driving?" I could feel Harry itching to get a forensics team out there as soon as we could.

Sondra patted Miki's arm again. "See, my friend, I told you the best thing you could do was come and talk to Harry and Zoe."

"You did exactly the right thing, Miki, and we appreciate you coming in. Every bit of information we can come up with has the potential to help, and you never know what might be vital to the investigation. So don't ever hesitate, okay?"

Miki agreed. Harry left but soon was back with a map of the park, and Miki pointed out exactly where her car had been parked and exactly where the motorcycle had been. Even though Harry and I both probed, Miki could add nothing new. The two women rose to leave. I gave both of them our cards with our cell phone numbers. "Call if you think of anything else. Call anytime." The two women walked out, and I turned back to the park map.

I went over in my mind what Miki had just told me, and something nagged at the back corner of my mind. What was I missing?

Harry rubbed his hands together. "I'll talk to Lianne if you'll call CSU and see if they can send out a team to meet us out at Mansfield Park. There's got to be tire tracks and who knows what else?"

"Just looking at the map, the distance could be perfect for a sniper. Something like two, three hundred yards," I said.

"Okay, we'll get things rolling here, then you and I are taking a trip back out to the scene. Let's just hope to hell we find some useful evidence." Harry's voice held a hint of excitement. He was silent for a moment, lost in thought. "Hey, didn't one of those firemen you talked to over at the fire tower mention a motorcycle?"

"Yes. One of the cadet firemen, more of an offhand remark." I rubbed my scratchy eyes. That's what I had forgotten. Someone at the academy scene had mentioned a motorcycle. "Forensics went over there. I know they went up in the tower looking for evidence of a sniper. Shell casings, finger prints, but I don't know if anyone looked for any tire tracks. Do you want me to go out there first and see what I can find out?"

"No, we can check later. But I do think nailing down

some details can go a long way to defuse things."

"Oh. You getting some heat?" I asked.

"Lianne is. She has the chief and the city manager and the mayor calling every hour to see if any progress has been made. Sheesh . . . Snipers killing female cops, and it just happens to be on my watch. In my town."

"I think the whole department feels that way."

Harry bared his teeth, but it wasn't a smile. "I want this sack of shit. I want him bad."

In Remembrance:

Thomas Wayne Birtrong, 31, (August 23, 1974) Officer Thomas Birtrong was killed in a traffic collision at 15th and Trinity Street while responding to an officer's call for assistance. Officer Birtrong's patrol car was operating "Code 3"—lights flashing and siren on—when the collision occurred.

(Austin City Connection -
The Official Web site of the City of Austin)

Chapter Ten

◆ ◆ ◆

"Harry, I'm taking my car," I said as we walked outside. "Not interested in drag racing anyone this morning."

"Okay," he said.

"I don't understand what it is with you men, you get behind the wheel and you think—"

"Zoe? I said okay. You drive." Harry's voice teasing.

"Good, I can skip giving you the lecture."

"Fine, I've heard it all before." He got in when I unlocked the Chevy's door, and we both fastened our seat belts.

"Besides, you're mainly just talking to hear yourself talk," he said. "As my momma used to say, if you were a two-bit radio, I'd turn you off."

I sat with my lip zipped. I was not going to give him the satisfaction.

We stopped at the first place we could find that sold cappuccinos. Both of us ordered a mocha. When I discovered the place had a little pastry section, I realized I'd never eaten breakfast. I grabbed some Danish and pecan rolls.

"Sugar and caffeine, what a way to start the day." I got back into the car, handing Harry the sack.

"Keeps us young." Harry laughed.

"Yeah, but it could cause us to die young."

"Nope, only the good die young . . . you and I will live to a ripe old age."

"Speak for yourself, Buster. I'm always good."

"Only when you're sleeping. Only when you're sleeping."

I have no idea why Harry and I get into silly moods. Sugar highs, most likely, I think.

The drive out to Lake Travis was uneventful, and the sunny, blue Texas sky was filled with fluffy white clouds. The live and burl oaks and Chinese elms had turned yellow, gold and orange. We don't have frost very often in Central Texas, and since we don't have the fabulous leaf colors of other areas, what little we do have is lovely. It just seldom gets cold enough early enough for Jack Frost to do any leaf painting this far south.

Two CSU technicians had reached the park before us and were waiting at the entrance kiosk. We discovered the LCRA Rangers had done as requested and closed the park the evening before. They were busy turning back some irate patrons bent on enjoying the summertime weather even though it was late September.

Days like today were made for loafing, camping, fishing, boating, but certainly not for investigating the death of a young woman who'd been full of life a mere twenty-four hours before.

We got out and I introduced myself to the forensic technicians, Jim Massey and Gary Greyson.

Massey, a tall thin, black guy with a shaved head, and a gold nose ring greeted Harry with a smile. They'd worked cases before. Greyson was a nerdy looking, pale white guy who reminded me of the after pictures of a strict weight loss program but one without exercise. His clothes were baggy and even his skin looked saggy. He'd worked with Harry before also.

Harry clued them in on what Miki Bellah had told us. We then all got back into our respective vehicles and drove over to the boat parking area. We parked in what we thought was the exact spot where Miki's car had been parked.

The four of us got out and looked at the area, trying to visualize the best place for a sniper to hide.

"Miki said she saw the motorcycle driving over near where that concession store is," Harry said, pointing in that direction.

"Maybe by that playground?" I asked.

"I think that's too far away even for a sniper," Greyson said. "That's probably four hundred or more yards away."

"Well, there's not many more places where he could have hidden," Massey said. His voice was a deep baritone.

"What about the bathroom?" I asked.

"Nope. Too easy to be caught or seen in there," said Harry.

"What about that dumpster area over there by the bathroom?" Massey pointed. "There's a fence around it."

"Yeah, it looks likely," said Harry. "It's about seventy-five to one hundred yards from where the victim was found. And it also looks like there's plenty of room to hide a motorcycle," Harry added. We all walked up the grassy slope to the fenced area.

It was not a dumpster location, but as we neared the spot, we could see some sort of a huge electrical box. Probably the power source for all the parking lot lighting. The transformer or whatever was painted a dark green and there were large cables running out of the top and up a creosote pole. The fenced in area was about a ten by ten size. Plenty large enough for a motorcycle or even several motorcycles to be parked inside the fenced area. Only a little grass grew in the area and the remainder was dirt, gravel and some concrete directly under the pole and electrical box. Harry and I stood back while the techs got busy searching, shining a bright flashlight on the ground.

"I think I see a tire track here," said Gary Massey. He opened his kit and pulled out some white powder . . . plaster, I assumed. He began making a plaster cast of the suspicious tire track. From where I stood, it didn't look like anything to me. But these guys were experts at finding even the faintest track or spot or print.

"We'll go every inch in here," the techs said in unison.

"What can we do?" asked Harry.

"Go with Jim back over to where the body was found," Gary said. "Expand the search area and see if there are any boot prints, and we'll get casts of everything."

Harry asked if they'd heard about the missing butterfly tattoo. They had and were as shocked as we were. Harry, Massey and I headed towards the bench and water area.

"We know now that he must have gone over here after shooting her in order to strip that tattoo off her body." Harry had a sick look on his face.

"Then he's left some trace of himself here," said Jim. "He can't be here without leaving something."

"Everybody walked around over there," I said.

"We can eliminate most footprints . . . all the sneakers and women's size shoes. What we're looking for now is a motorcycle boot print," said Jim.

"How do you know he wore that type of boot and wasn't wearing sneakers?" I asked.

"Remember you told us that lady named Miki said the bike was big, black and evil-looking?"

"Yeah, that's what she said."

"That tells me the guy was dressed in motorcycle

clothes, and if you wear the clothes, then you definitely wear the boots."

"Oh." What do I know about motorcycles and their accessories? Zip. Nada. That's why I'm glad we have forensics people around.

Harry and Jim had begun their search around the parameter of the concrete patio area and were bent over inspecting even the concrete, shining flashlights. They kept expanding the area. After some minutes, Harry called Jim over to look at a spot in the dirt that was several feet away.

"All right," said Jim. "I gotcha now, dude."

"You found something already?" I asked as I joined them.

"A boot print," said Jim.

"Man, y'all are good," I said.

"Just great detective work," said Harry. "You'll learn how to do this stuff one day, Zoe. Especially if you keep hanging around with me."

"I know, Harry. You're the best."

"And don't you forget it."

Jim began making a plaster cast of the faint boot print.

I walked back up the slope to see whether his partner had finished with his tire track. Gary was loading their van with the plaster of the tire track. "If we're lucky, this is good enough that we can get the tire brand, and that will help us identify the motorcycle."

"You can do that?" I asked.

"Yep, there's these new software programs that identify tire tracks. Pretty cool, huh?"

I agreed that it was.

"The CSI television shows have helped increase the awareness of technology that's available," Gary said, "and it's lots easier to get funding for new stuff now."

"Once we know the make, then we can start checking local dealers for a bike fitting that tire?" I said.

Jim and Harry came to the van with Jim carefully carrying the boot print cast. I watched as Jim stowed it properly inside their van.

Gary went back into the fenced area, and I peeked in to see what he might be doing. I've been to a few crime scenes but am still learning the intricacies of forensics.

"I'm looking right here where I think he sat on his motorcycle and watched the victim through his rifle scope." Gary looked over at me, his round face covered in sweat. "By the way, has she been identified absolutely yet? I like to call victims by their names so I always remember who I'm working for. I don't like to ever forget who my victim was and what was done to him or her. That makes it easier for me to keep focused and easier for me to catch their killer."

"Miss Bethany Mayfield," Harry answered before I could.

Harry always showed victims the greatest respect by calling them Mister or Miss or Mrs. I admired him more for that.

"And Miss Bethany Mayfield was on the job?" Gary Greyson asked.

"She was a patrol officer. But she was on vacation. She was not on duty when she was shot," I said.

"Makes no difference to me if it was line of duty or not. She's one of ours, right?" Greyson's round face held a grim look.

"Right," said Harry.

"I do believe that's a fiber snagged right there." Gary pointed to two thin brown threads that were almost invisible.

The man has eagle eyes, I thought. Great for our side.

He plucked the fibers with tweezers and popped them into a plastic bag.

"Slowly, slowly, we're building our case against this scumbag," said Gary Greyson.

That statement needed no comment, I thought.

As I walked back over to the body's chalk outline on the limestone boulders, I looked at the water and wondered if we'd ever find this sniper. I knew I could count on Harry putting in all the extra time and effort possible and knew I would, too. Would it be enough?

It *had* to be.

Chapter Eleven

◆　◆　◆

He sat at his computer and looked at the slut's pictures and immediately got sick to his stomach. How could these women do such nasty things? Had they no pride—no shame?

My Elena, would never have allowed anyone to see her like this. She was the most beautiful girl he had ever seen. She took care of him when Papa beat him. She'd clean and doctor the cuts Papa's belt had made as he struck his buttocks and legs.

Elena made sure he had clean clothes to wear to school each day. She knew Mama would be sunk into her vodka bottle and never do the washing or ironing. She'd bring fried chicken or tacos or burgers home from her job to feed him. He loved his sister, but suddenly one day she moved away, and he was left alone with them. The parents from hell.

Why did Elena leave? He had loved her so. But how could he blame her? There was nothing good for her in that old house. But he thought she loved him and would always keep him safe. He was not safe after Elena left. His Papa beat him more, and his Mama caught him with his hand on his groin one night and tried to cut off his manhood. "Nasty, dirty," Mama said. "You are the nastiest boy I have ever seen."

At least Papa stopped her from doing that. But he had to go to the hospital, and Mama had to go to that bad place. Papa and I were pretty much okay until Mama got out.

Then he saw those nasty pictures of Elena on the computer at the library. Some boys were looking at her and talking about what they'd like to do to her.

Those nasty, dirty pictures of Elena. But deep in his heart, in his secret place, he loved seeing how beautiful her body was. How perfectly her breasts were shaped with the dark brown nipples and how enticing they looked on the computer screen. How dark her pubic hair was and how pink the skin was underneath. And that sexy blue and black butterfly tattoo on her left buttocks. He longed to kiss that butterfly spot. But how nasty, dirty she was. Nastiest girl he had ever seen.

In Remembrance:

Leland Dale Anderson, 26, (June 6, 1975)
Officer Leland Anderson was killed when he was attacked by three men at the intersection of Eighth Street and Congress Avenue. Officer Anderson had observed one of the subjects selling papers and had stopped to check if he was in compliance with City ordinances. When Officer Anderson attempted to arrest one of the men on outstanding traffic warrants, a fight ensued. One of the subjects gained control of Officer Anderson's gun and shot him. Despite Officer Anderson's bulletproof vest, one bullet entered between the front and rear panel and penetrated his chest. The subjects were arrested following a pursuit in which gunfire was exchanged.

(Austin City Connection -
The Official Web site of the City of Austin)

Chapter Twelve

◆ ◆ ◆

Harry and I headed back into town. Neither of us talked much, our minds too full of questions. Of who was doing this and why. Who wanted to kill young policewomen? Was it a vendetta against the women themselves or a vendetta against the police or what?

What we had were pieces of twine and if we pulled this one, we might get lucky. On the other hand, if we pulled that piece of twine, we had bupkus. We needed to find the right string to pull.

When we got back to headquarters, we passed by two officers heading to the garage. "The Commander wants to see you, Harry," one of them said.

Harry and I walked into the Commander's office. "Lianne?" said Harry.

"This is a formal meeting, Detective Albright," Lianne said, her voice stiff.

Harry had not noticed the other people in the room, but I had. Two men, dressed formally in dark suits, white shirts and dark ties. They also wore black, highly polished shoes. That was my first clue that things were about to get dicey.

The commander's office was rather small so that by the time we walked in and added to the body count, the room was packed. Lianne sat behind her desk and everyone else stood. She motioned for Harry and I to be seated, but we both elected to stand.

Commander Crowder introduced us to FBI agents, Craig Reed and Lonnie Argent. "These gentlemen work for the Bureau's Violent Crimes Unit, and since we now have two police officers killed by a sniper, the Chief thought we should consult with the FBI."

"Are we turning the case over to them?" I asked. I stepped forward a bit until I was partially in front of Harry because I had a feeling he would overreact.

"No," said Lianne. "Of course not."

"You are still in charge," said one of the FBI agents. I didn't have it straight in my head which one was which.

"We're strictly here to advise and to help in whatever way we can," the other guy said.

I heard Harry behind me take in a sharp breath, and I stepped back and mashed his foot with mine before he could say anything. He was lucky I wore sneakers.

"Great," I said. "And do you have any insights or thoughts to give us?" I asked the agents in a polite tone.

"Look," said the older of the two, "we don't want to step on any jurisdictional toes here, but—"

"Let's see what we can do with our combined resources," finished the other agent.

How did they do that? I wondered.

I also needed to get who was who straight in my mind before much more time had passed, otherwise we'd be saying "Hey you" all day, and I don't like to work that way.

"Okay. That sounds fair, Argent?" I looked at the younger one.

"I'm Lon Argent," the older one said. He looked to be about an inch shorter than my five feet nine inches, but his dark charcoal suit made him look taller. He had hazel-colored eyes, almost hidden by black rim glasses. His crew cut reddish-blond hair did nothing for his receding hairline. "Call me Lonnie."

"Then that makes you, Reed," Harry said to the other agent.

"Craig Reed." Craig's dark hair was cut Marine Corps short, and his eyes were nearly black. His body inside the dark grey suit looked well muscled, as if he worked out on a regular basis. "Look, we honestly don't want to cause any problems. We're just concerned about this sniper and want to do all we can to help capture him. If you'll let us see what you've found out, we can pool our information."

"Yeah, right," breathed Harry.

"May I suggest we go get some coffee," I said. "We'd definitely like to hear what y'all have discovered. Sharing information can only help us. We'll see you at Starbucks over at the American One Center in about twenty minutes."

"That's 600 Congress, right?" Argent confirmed. The FBI agents agreed and they left. As soon as they had cleared the door, Harry turned to Lianne. "What are we supposed to do with those peckerwoods?"

"Cooperation would be nice, Harry," said Lianne.

"Ha! Every time I've tried to cooperate with the Feebs I got my butt in a sling."

"Harry, maybe you're getting too old. Things have changed. I've worked with the Feds on more than one case, and we've had a good relationship." Lianne came over to where Harry stood.

She didn't bat her green eyes, but I saw a subtle change in Harry's face. Lianne had that effect on men. Up close, she looked prettier than you had at first thought. Yet now that she was in a command position, she did things to

117

downplay her looks. Smoothing her auburn curls in a French twist and adding nothing special to her face. She didn't need make up, thanks to a Castilian Spanish grandmother. Her face was one of those without blemishes, wrinkles, or large pores. She wore simple suits, which on most people would have hidden their figure but somehow enhanced hers. If I didn't love her like a sister, I would have hated her.

"You're a political animal, Lianne," I said. "That's one of your strong points. That's why you're in charge of this department and on the fast track to move up in the department."

Harry smiled, "That and the fact that she's a top notch investigator. Of course, you know, she learned everything from me."

Lianne and I laughed. "Naturally," we said in unison.

"Okay, we'll try to work with these guys and hope they'll tell us whatever they find out," Harry grumbled something else I couldn't hear.

"That's all that I expect," said Lianne. "Let's just catch this scuzzbag and get him off the street immediately if not sooner."

Argent and Reed were sitting in their unmarked car when we got to Starbucks.

The four of us walked inside, and, after picking up our order, we found a back corner table. Harry handed over a folder. "This is really all we have right now." I knew the file had not been updated with the information we'd received today. But I also knew Harry wasn't about to give the Feds everything.

The agents quickly read it and Reed said, "That's it?"

"What do you guys have?" I asked.

"We got a palm print from that shooting out at the

academy," said Lonnie. "From the fire tower. We don't know if it belongs to the shooter, but we're hopeful."

I thought Harry would choke on his coffee. He would give someone holy hell because we didn't get that from CSU.

Lonnie pretended not to notice. "And we've found out one of the firemen cadets left the door unlocked."

Then Craig Reed spoke up. He had a soft voice, with a slight accent that I couldn't place . . . Deep South someplace. "Some fireman cadet thought he saw a motorcycle out there around the time of the shooting."

Argent's eyes hadn't missed the look Harry and I gave each other. "What?" he asked.

I remembered how one of the firemen cadets mentioned how he thought he'd heard a motorcycle the day Ramona Sanchez was killed. I wished I had followed up on it immediately when we first thought of it, but we needed to get out to Mansfield Park.

"We just got some information right before we met with y'all that points to a guy on a motorcycle," said Harry, looking down his large nose at these Feds. "That's not in our folder. We hadn't had time to write it up yet."

"Do you know what kind of bike it was?" asked Reed.

I looked at Harry and waited for him to speak.

"Our CSU techs got a tire track," Harry said. "Out at that Mansfield dam park."

"Hey, that's great," said Reed. "We've got a computer program that can identify tires and tell which bike they would be on and—"

"Our bike has been identified as an YZF-R1 Yamaha." Argent grinned a wolfish grin. "If we can connect that one to yours out at the dam—"

"Finding out what kind of motorcycle would be a big

step forward in our investigation," I said. Harry looked like he wanted to throttle me, but I thought it was a big break in the case, and I wasn't about to let that pass by. "If we can get our CSU to copy a photo of our tire track, can we e-mail it to you?"

"That'll do," said Argent. "And we'll send you ours along with that palm print that our forensics team's new light equipment found."

So that's why we didn't know about the palm print. The FBI Crime Investigative Unit obviously had more sophisticated equipment than our guys.

Since there was nothing more to add, we parted after handshakes all around.

Harry and I walked to my car. "I thought that went well," I said, letting sarcasm into my voice.

"Well, you could have just given our whole case away right there."

"Harry, what does it matter if we share the information? We want to catch this guy, and, if the Feds can help . . . then I see nothing wrong. They gave us as much as we gave them."

"You don't understand—"

"No, I don't think you understand." I stopped and got right up in Harry's face—eyeball to eyeball. "Times have changed. Your attitude is outdated and old-fashioned," I said.

"Maybe you think they've changed, but Feebs don't change. Those two would like nothing more than to take our case from us."

"And your point being what?"

Harry shrugged and I continued. "If the murderer gets stopped, what difference does it make if we do it or if they do it? Is it the publicity? You crave the publicity?"

"You know better than that."

"Then what?"

"You need to be the one who cracks this case. It'll help you move up in the department."

"Good grief!" I said. "How do you know I even want to move up?"

Harry looked at me like I'd just lost my mind.

"Okay," I said. "Of course I want to move up, but stopping this sniper is priority one, and if we lose out to the Feds, it won't hurt my feelings none. The next case will come up and we'll solve it. But in the meantime, this sniper scuzz will be off the street, and some of my fellow officers will still be alive."

Harry was quiet for about three minutes. I was worried that he was going to blow his stack, but I was totally wrong. "You're right, Zoe. The main thing is to take this freaking A-hole down and take him down good enough to send him to Huntsville. Of course he'll get out in ten years for being a good boy."

"There is a bright side."

"Oh yeah?" Harry wanted to know.

"With the Feds in on the case, he'll most likely go to federal prison. No parole."

He laughed. "Damn straight. That is a bright side."

We decided the next thing we needed to do was to talk to all our academy cadet witnesses and firemen cadets again to see if anyone remembered anything besides the motorcycle. Maybe now we'd get more details.

We went back out to the APD Academy and talked to every police cadet again—asking each if anyone had seen or heard anything. None of them could add to the puzzle.

We got a list of the firemen cadets and went over to the fire tower. Two fire cadets we spoke with remembered seeing a black and chrome motorcycle out there the day Ramona Sanchez had been shot. Another couple of them remembered hearing the bike leaving shortly after the shooting. It was gratifying to verify some pieces of the puzzle. Even if it was only the corner edge pieces. Unfortunately, this new information only confirmed what we already knew, nothing new was added, and that was a bit disheartening. We were at a definite standstill.

We were both exhausted by the time we wrapped it up and started back home. I needed to drop by Cynthia's and find out about Byron. I needed to see my husband and make sure he was really okay. He needed to be back at the nursing home.

My being torn in two different directions was getting to be a bit too much to take.

In Remembrance:

Ralph A. Ablanedo, 26, (May 18, 1978)
Officer Ralph Ablanedo was killed in the line of duty during a traffic stop in the 900 block of Live Oak Street. Officer Ablanedo had ticketed the driver of the car, Sheila Meinert, for driving without a license, then ran a routine check on the passenger, David Lee Powell, who had warrants for misdemeanor theft and hot checks. As Officer Ablanedo spoke on his radio, Powell opened fire with a fully automatic AK-47, penetrating Officer Ablanedo's bulletproof vest. Despite his injuries, Officer Ablanedo was able to give officers a description of the car before he lost consciousness and died. Powell opened fire on a second officer when he was stopped a short time later, and also tossed a hand grenade, which failed to explode. His companion, Meinert, surrendered, and Powell fled on foot, only to be arrested a few hours later after an extensive manhunt. Powell was eventually convicted of murder and sentenced to death.

(Austin City Connection -
The Official Web site of the City of Austin)

Chapter Thirteen

◆ ◆ ◆

Once again, there was no one at Cynthia's house, but I found a neighbor in one of the apartment complexes nearby who knew her. She said Cynthia and Lucy had moved to a house they had just bought. She rummaged in her file drawer and came up with what she thought was their address out near Burnet Road along with a phone number.

I called the phone number as I drove over.

"Ms. Barrow, Byron is fine," Cynthia Martin said when I reached her. "I'm sorry we scareded you but I was afeared of that Nurse Foster. The way she talked, if any of them patients acted up or made noise, she'd take care of them permanently. I couldn't take a chance with Mr. Byron or Mr. and Mrs. T."

"Okay. But I need to know where you are and where is my husband."

She verified the address I had, but then my phone went dead again. Darn battery, I think it's losing its memory or whatever. Sure hated to buy a new one but it looked as if I had no choice.

I looked up and realized I was only a half-mile away from Cynthia's. The house was in a neighborhood just west of North Lamar. When I drove into the driveway, Cynthia came outside to meet me.

Cynthia is a little slip of womanhood, but strong and

wiry. I've seen her lift a patient almost twice her size. She always used leverage and her legs and never seemed to put any strain on her back. She was in her mid-thirties, with dark hair and eyes, and skin the color of milk chocolate. Anytime Byron was agitated, she could always soothe and calm him.

She and I had formed a sort of friendship over the months since Byron had moved into Pecan Grove and I trusted her instincts.

"He's here Miz Zoe," Cynthia said. "And he's perfectly fine."

"You know you gave me quite a scare."

"I know, Miz, but I felt—" she said.

"Like you had no choice, right?"

I followed her inside and stopped just inside the door. Cynthia and Lucy had converted a living room and a dining room into one large patient bedroom. They had hospital beds. And a wheelchair and a bedside potty, and each bed had a privacy curtain. I could smell the fresh paint and everything was spotless.

Byron was in a bed by a window. His bed had a rainbow-striped spread and pillowcase to match. An ivy plant hung from the ceiling near the window.

"Cynthia this all looks a bit like perhaps you planned it," I said. "Like it had nothing to do with Pecan Groves and Miss Foster."

"I know how it looks, but believe me, this was not the plan," Cynthia said. "My plan was to discuss things with you in a week or two when everything was ready here, and if you agreed, you'd consent to moving Mr. Byron over here to live."

Sam T. was in the middle bed, with bed linens that matched Byron and Virginia T. was in the far bed. Her bed linens were pastel geometric patterns, definitely feminine looking. Her area also had a privacy screen that folded up and stood next to the wall. Both Thielepapes could move enough and were aware enough to help when moved from bed to wheelchair or onto one of the large recliners near their beds.

Lucy was just smoothing the covers on Sam T.'s bed and said "Hi," then she hurried off towards the back. I could see a kitchen back there. I wasn't surprised—Lucy was the shy one.

"You wanted to try to keep them here?" I asked.

"After that happened out at Pecan Grove, I thought this would be best. Just until we can find a good place for them. A safe place," Cynthia said.

I walked inside the bedroom and over to Byron's bed. He looked as if he were asleep. And he was clean, and I could tell he'd been cared for even better than when he was at Pecan Groves.

"I don't know, Cynthia. Looks like you're taking good care of them, but don't you have to be licensed or something? Who is going to do physical therapy on Byron? And speech therapy on Sam T.?"

"We can get visiting therapists. I've already made the phone calls to start."

"And what about their meals and medications? The responsibilities here are huge and what if one of them gets very sick?"

"We can handle the food and the meds. We know what's needed. And we'd just call EMS and take them to the hospital if someone gets sick. That's the same thing we'd do at the nursing home."

"But the help I get to pay for Byron's care, I doubt they'd approve of home care."

"Don't you and Mr. Barrow's parents pay?"

"Yes, along with my parents. I don't think my parents would argue about it, if I agreed to keep him here. But the Barrows are going to protest, I'm sure."

"Even if we just do it until you can find a place for him?"

"Okay, Cynthia. I'll see about finding a new nursing home and in the meantime, I'll do what I can to see if you can get licensed or whatever is necessary for a home health care place."

"I'd appreciate it, Miz Zoe. This is something I've thought about and planned for months and when the new administration at Pecan Grove took over, I just thought I had to get them out of there. I wish I could have taken three or four more. These three are my favorites. I couldn't let them die."

"Were you at the duplex first?" I asked.

"At first, I took them to my place—the duplex. My sister, who had just moved in there, had a hissy fit. Said I was going to get arrested and she wasn't going to jail over sumpin' I did."

"Lucy and I won ten thousand dollars on a lottery ticket, can you believe? We've probably spent five hundred and never won until this past July. I had already applied for a loan for this house and it came through. We stayed at the duplex for two days until my friend, Dave, and Lucy's uncle, Bob could finish up the paint and repairs in here. This house just wasn't ready yet."

Cynthia began crying. "I couldn't leave my patients there to be mistreated or even worse."

"It's okay, Cynthia. We'll take care of everything. Don't you worry."

"Thank you, Miz Barrow." She patted Byron's shoulder and walked over to check on her other two patients, then headed back to the kitchen.

I pulled the privacy curtain around Byron's bed. "Are you okay, honey?" I asked my husband. He wasn't thrashing around or restless which is how he can get sometimes when he's overtired or uncomfortable. He seemed to be in great shape, and that was all I wanted to know. That he was okay.

I adjusted his pillow and said, "You gave me a bit of a scare, sneaking out like that." He didn't answer. He never responds, but the doctors say they honestly don't know how much he might understand. I think he understands comforting sounds. I hope he understood loving sounds. I continued touching him, rubbing my hand over his dark hair, which we kept cut short for easier care, assuring myself that he was indeed totally okay.

I used Cynthia's phone to put in a call to Byron's doctor, Dr. Foster, and told her what had happened.

"I heard some patients had been moved," Dr. Foster chuckled after hearing the whole story. "Give me the address, and I'll drop by tomorrow and check on Byron. And Zoe, you sound like you need some rest."

I said I'd be fine and hung up the phone and sat holding my husband's hand. I kept making soothing sounds of conversation with Byron as his blue-green eyes were open, but, as usual, there was no light in them.

No one could ever understand how hard it was to see him like this . . . here, but not really here. When I heard about the remark Nancy Regan had once made when someone asked how she was doing, I could relate. Mrs. Regan replied along these lines, "I'm okay for a woman who's sitting here all alone with my husband who is six feet away."

I'd been in love with Byron Barrow since I was nineteen-years-old. A rebellion bug bite, along with a highly organized and smothering mother, got me into hot water in high school. Playing basketball my sophomore and junior years, with an eye on a basketball scholarship at the University of Texas with the Lady Longhorns held me somewhat in check. Then a twisted knee and my smart mouth soon got me expelled my senior year. I dropped out and went to work.

I spent evenings hanging out with fellow dropouts, drinking beer and smoking an occasional joint. One evening, we were in front of a convenience store hassling customers when this sexy looking police officer with tight buns drove up and broke up the party. The store manager had called in to complain about the "gang" of kids outside. Everyone's parents were called and the kids sent home, except for me. My parents weren't home, so Patrol Officer Byron Barrow drove me home and waited with me until Herb and Helene Taylor got back.

That was about the same time I was realizing that I wasn't cut out to be a fast-food waitress. I took my GED, settled down and entered college. A short time later, Byron called and asked me out. He'd been keeping an eye on me, and he was hoping I would straighten out on my own, because he'd fallen in love with me that first night.

From then on, we were inseparable and got married a short time later. I got a degree in criminal justice and joined the Austin Police Academy. Our lives were exactly as we wanted except for children, which we planned for later, never dreaming a gangbanger named Jesse Garcia would shatter that dream with his bullet.

Now I fill my life with work. Dinner with my folks when I have to. Fortunately, Herb and Helene Taylor are retired and travel a lot so I don't have to deal with my mother. I love Helene, but I can never please her. She is the great goddess of organization and she expects me to be like her. I try, but I can never measure up to her standards. I could spend days with my father and enjoy his company every minute.

Byron's family is not my choice for a fun evening either. I see them when I have to and I try not to have to.

My brother, Chip and his family are nearby and I see them often, but they're busy and I'm busy. The remainder of my time is spent with pals from APD or I do things on my own. I don't mind being alone, but I miss that constant companionship of my loving husband.

So I kept holding Byron's hand and telling him how my investigation was going and did my best to deal with my situation.

"What exactly happened over at Pecan Grove?" I asked Cynthia when she returned to Byron's room.

"The new owners were cutting our hours and our pay. Told us we'd get shares of stock instead of an increase in salary. Big flippin' deal. That stock ain't gonna feed my kids. But to make matters even worse, by cutting our hours we could see they're going to be short-staffed and we felt our patients would be the ones to suffer."

"Okay, I can understand that and even agree things were not good. But to just walk out with the patients seems a bit extreme. You didn't think anything could be worked out? Maybe contact each of the families and get our loved ones moved?"

"Did you meet that Ms. Foster?"

"Yes, I met her."

"She told us she expected us to medicate all the patients early in the evening so that she could get her paperwork done." Cynthia was pacing the room, very obviously angry with Ms. Foster. "That all important paperwork was what brought in the money to operate the facility she said, and she'd be dammed if she'd let those demanding patients interrupt her work."

"Well, she was so intent on her work that she didn't even know any of the patients were missing," I said. "She barely even spoke to me, even when I demanded answers from her. I had to force her to call her boss."

"She also told us she knew the best way to cope with demanding patients was to give them a sleep aid, and if necessary, she would give even a stronger dose," Cynthia said.

"You mean like euthanize them?"

"That's not exactly what she said, but you sure knew that's what she meant." Cynthia's eyes flashed, and I knew she was upset over that idea.

"I think," I told Cynthia, "we have enough information so that we can get an investigation going over there and, hopefully, any corrections will be taken care of by the authorities."

"You don't want us to go back over there, do you?" Cynthia asked.

"I just want Byron to be taken care of properly, and I know you will do that. But there are some insurance problems. I do get help with his physical therapy and a couple of other medical things. But he has to be in an approved nursing facility." I hugged Cynthia. "And you may have some legal problems. The police had to be called in because the patients were gone. I don't know what could happen there. I'll do my best to help you, but you may have to give up your dream of your own nursing home for now."

"I hadn't even thought of no legal ramifications."

"I'll do what I can to get you out of hot water. But I'm also going to have to insist your patients are placed back into a licensed care center . . . the sooner the better."

Cynthia wiped her eyes and hugged me again. It was time for me to go. I kissed my husband goodbye. I didn't notice the wetness on my own cheek until I got into my car.

In Remembrance:

Lee Craig Smith, 28, (December 15, 1979)
Officer Lee Smith, a motorcycle officer, died as a result of injuries suffered in an accident while on duty. While pursuing a motorist on the newly completed Mopac freeway, Officer Smith lost control of his motorcycle. A defective steering part caused the accident. Although Officer Smith had seemingly recovered from his injuries, he died suddenly at his home some months later as a result of the accident.
(Austin City Connection -
The Official Web site of the City of Austin)

Chapter Fourteen

◆ ◆ ◆

I slept hard once I got to bed—no dreams, no nocturnal restlessness. When the alarm went off at seven, I banged it off and went back to sleep. At seven forty-five, Harry was knocking on my door. I let him in and stumbled to the bathroom to shower. I used the blow dryer on my hair and then used the curling iron to give a lift to the top.

I inspected my face in my lighted make-up mirror. Even though I had a few new wrinkle lines, my skin looked fairly good. I applied a minimum of make-up and joined Harry in my kitchen. The kitchen was long and narrow, but ended in a breakfast nook with bay windows. That part of the room reminded me of my grandmother's kitchen in Fort Worth, and was a huge factor in my leasing this place. That and the back deck with its view of Town Lake and the city of Austin itself.

He was sitting at the table in the breakfast nook, drinking coffee, eating eggs and looking completely rested although I knew he'd had no more sleep than I. "How do you manage this. You're twelve years older than me."

"Only ten," he said.

"Whatever."

"It's all my clean living," he said. "Good diet, good exercise . . . early to bed, early to rise—"

I snorted. "Oh yeah. All the doughnuts and coffee—"

"Double bacon cheeseburgers and curly fries and tacos and chicken-fried steak—"

"Well, I eat all that, too and I don't have your energy, but I'll try to keep up."

"I got a call from CSU this morning," he said without another comment on aging or rest. "They did find a decent fingerprint out at the Mansfield park site."

"Okay, does that help us in some way?" I yawned, but not on purpose.

"Would knowing it's a palm print instead of a fingerprint excite you?"

"If we could find the palm that matches, maybe so." I admit to being a little slow on putting things together. My experience with the repeat offenders unit on dealing drugs was totally different than homicide. But finally I got it. "The Feds found a palm print in the fire tower. If those two match then we've got the same scumbag at both locations, don't we?"

Harry was grinning. He had a look somewhat like I've seen on Lyric's face when my cat brings me a dead bug. "And if our fingerprint people can't identify, then perhaps the Feds can. They have access to more databases than we do. We might come up with the name of a suspect even quicker."

"What? You've got more?" I poured myself some coffee, thankful that he'd made it, and I toasted two English muffins.

"Remember the butterfly tattoos on both victims?" I nodded and he continued. "CSU has tracked down the most likely place—"

"Not the exact place, huh?" I asked.

"—and it's a good source and contact for us to find out who inked them." Harry wiped his mouth as he finished up his eggs over medium.

"So that's got to be our first stop this morning."

"Yep. Annie Frannie's Tattoo Parlor on Interstate Thirty-five and Sixth Street."

"That's just down the road from where we're sitting."

"Why do you think I stopped in here? We'll go as soon as you finish."

The remainder of my food was gone as quickly as I could eat without choking. I'd finish my coffee in the car.

"Let's rock and roll, Zoe," he said.

In Remembrance:

Robert Martinez Jr., 26, (February 25, 1989)
Officer Robert Martinez Jr. was killed in the line of duty when his patrol car struck a tree. Martinez, who was en route to assist another officer, swerved to avoid a pick up truck that had pulled into his path. At the time of the collision, Officer Martinez was working the last hour of his last shift before a scheduled transfer to Walking Beat.

(Austin City Connection -
The Official Web site of the City of Austin)

Chapter Fifteen

Harry insisted on driving this morning and with his usual driving attitude, pushed the Crown Victoria hard and shot off the Interstate. We cruised Sixth Street that, if I remember correctly, was originally named Pecan. All the streets running east and west in Austin were named after trees when the town was laid out. I'm not exactly sure when the tree streets were changed to numbers. History was never my strong point anyway.

I've heard from friends who were around Austin at the time Sixth Street became an entertainment district. They told of how in the mid-seventies a man opened a blues club on Sixth, naming it Antone's after himself, and for a good ten years, several blocks of Sixth teemed with clubs and bands playing live original music. Johnny Winter was a big influence on the local scene by recording an LP at The Vulcan Gas Company (I think this was a nightclub) on Congress Avenue.

Early performers along about this time were Stevie Ray Vaughan who played as guitarist with The Triple Threat, and Lou Ann Barton doing vocals. Jimmy Vaughan and Kim Wilson started The Fabulous Thunderbirds. Some rock and roll bands back then were Jesse Sublett and the Skunks, Jellyroll, and The Violators—an all girl band except they included Jesse Sublett. Of course, Willie Nelson and

Jerry Jeff Walker were on the local scene, too. Sixth Street was the reason Austin became known as the live music capital of the world.

I did know that many of the historic buildings along East Sixth Street date back to the 1800s and early 1900s. And there's been talk in recent years to play up these Victorian architecture beauties and make Sixth Street the crown jewel of Austin. Interspersed with the numerous bars and clubs are tattoo parlors, casual cafes, upscale restaurants, and the elegant Driskill Hotel. Waller Creek passes through the tree-lined seven hundred block just off the highway.

One big Austin attraction is live music that runs the gamut from jazz, blues, and country to rock, hip-hop, and derivations of these. You will also find every kind of food, not only Texas specialties like chili, ribs, Bar-B-Q and Tex-Mex but also steak, seafood, Italian, Cajun cooking, and deli delights. While young and trendy are often used to describe the people who meander the street, you can also find yourself mingling with Hollywood's rich and famous, politicians, local and nationally known musicians, and scads of university students.

Halloween is a trip all its own as it brings out the lovely or scary along with the bizarre. Tourists visit Sixth Street routinely to see what it is that makes Austin weird. Major motto for Sixth Street is "anything goes." Or perhaps its motto is the often seen slogan, "Keep Austin Weird." However, the music being played at the clubs has mostly turned into the same old and purists say the music died in Austin in the mid-eighties. In the past few yeas, however, the South by Southwest Music Festival has brought back original talent.

At one point, crime threatened to overtake the area, but strong efforts by club owners and the police have done a lot to clean up the world-renowned entertainment and tourism area. For now, the good guys are winning, but it's never easy.

Annie Frannie's Tattoo Parlor looked much neater and cleaner than I imagined. The owner, Annie Frannie herself, a gigantic woman of indeterminate age, noticed my inspection. "We have to be more careful nowadays because of AIDS," she said.

She wore a Hawaiian muumuu with the basic color being yellow, and yellow leather thongs were on her feet. About six bracelets dangled from both arms, while studs and loops of different colors and sizes lined both her ears. Her blonde hair was streaked with red, yellow, and blue and hung down her back in ringlets. She had a smile a mile wide.

Harry had a computer-generated photograph of the butterfly tattoo on both victims and handed it to Annie Frannie. "Yes, that's one of my designs," she said. "Do you have photos of the girls with the tattoos?"

Harry handed over cadet photos of both Ramona Sanchez and Bethany Mayfield.

Annie Frannie looked, turning the photos this way and that. Finally, she looked at us. "Yes. These two were in here. And I put the butterfly tattoos on them . . . left buttocks cheek of each girl."

"Did they come in alone?"

"As near as I can remember. But they didn't come in at the same time . . ." She rolled her eyes up, then closed them as she thought. "Yes, I'm sure each one came in alone. But there was something funny about it all."

Harry and I both looked at each other but remained silent. We didn't want to interrupt her thinking.

After a moment she said, "I recall a man called and made the appointment times for each woman. I don't usually work by appointment . . . this is strictly a walk-in business. That's why I remember these two. And he paid for each one, but he didn't come in with them."

"How did he pay?" I asked.

"Not by credit card. He had me send an invoice to him, and then he prepaid by money order," she said.

"And you went along with that," I asked.

"Yeah. Sometimes I surprise myself. What can I say? I liked his voice," she said.

"Do you have the name and address for this sexy voice?" I asked. "You know, from the invoice?"

"I'm sure I do, somewhere." She turned, heading towards the back. Once inside the small storage/office space, she rummaged in a gray metal file cabinet. Harry and I followed along and amused ourselves looking at the tattoo designs hanging all round the walls. After about five minutes or so, she came up with a receipt and a carbon of a money order. The name on the receipt was barely legible. And wouldn't you know it read . . . Jon Schmidt.

"John Smith, huh?"

"Oh, I didn't realize," Annie Frannie said.

"What about an address where you sent the invoice?" asked Harry.

She looked in the file cabinet another two and three minutes and found a copy of the invoice for Jon Schmidt. "Looks like it's an apartment. 4401 Speedway. Number 608."

"Okay," I said and we thanked her for her cooperation and left.

We drove over to Speedway and were not really surprised to find this was a post office mailbox store. A mailbox only for people who like to remain anonymous.

The lady in charge was named Robbie Serpico. She was

a slender lady with beautiful brown eyes who looked to be in her mid-to-late-fifties. She had a great smile that she turned on to Harry as soon as he walked in the door.

Harry flashed his badge, and Robbie got a twinkle in her eyes.

Even though Harry's a big guy, something about him could make some women want to cuddle him like a big teddy bear. Robbie fell into that category. Of course, it might not have been Harry's charm at all, some women just get a thrill when a police officer asks for help. Whatever rows your boat, I thought.

It only took a moment to realize I would be a hindrance to this situation, so I hung back, kept quiet, and let Harry handle the lady.

Harry leaned his elbows on the counter and flashed her his best, most charming smile. We could and would get a court order if necessary even though we really hated to make that much effort for such a small matter, he told her. Harry gave her another big smile when she decided it would be quicker and much nicer all around if she gave us any information she had on Box 608.

"Mr. Schmidt always pays cash and he pays six months in advance," Robbie said. She wore tan slacks and a brown and white striped shirt. Her clothes looked like a uniform, but she wore them with all the style of a New York fashion maven. Her light brown hair was cut short and highlighted.

"How do you contact him?" Harry asked.

"We just put a notice in his box when the rent is due."

"Does he come in to pay?"

"No, he mails me a money order."

"Where does he purchase those?"

"At different convenience stores. I have them all in my files."

"May I see them?" Harry wanted to know.

"I'm really not supposed to. I wasn't even supposed to give you any information, but I did. But I just can't hand over my files. They're confidential."

"I totally understand that," said Harry. "I tell you what. Why don't you leave that file drawer cracked open. Then you and I'll go over to that Starbucks next door. I'll buy you a cup of java and my partner can watch the desk for you."

His smile would have melted even the coldest heart. You old son of a gun, I thought. You've solved our problem with a little old-fashioned flirtation. Robbie nodded in agreement and Harry hustled her outside and next door before she could think about it.

I quickly opened the file drawer and found the manilla folder for Box 608. Robbie had told the truth. Jon Schmidt had sent money orders, and each one was from a different convenience store. I noticed he'd only had the box for a little over a year. As I thumbed through the earliest, one caught my eye. In the space where the buyer wrote his own name, part of the line had been marked out with ink. Maybe he put his real name instead of Jon Schmidt, I thought. I slipped that one in my pocket and closed the file drawer just as Harry and Robbie walked back inside.

I nodded to Harry and I walked outside. Harry joined me a few minutes later. "Well?" he asked.

"I got lucky. How about you?"

He flushed a light pinkish color. "Zoe, sometimes you're too nosy, you know that?"

"Comes with the territory. Come on, give. You going to see Robbie again?"

"Probably. Well, yes. I'm meeting her for a drink tonight. Just as a thank you for all her help."

"Of course. Line of duty and all that."

"Enough of this nonsense," he grinned. "What did you find out?"

When I explained about the marked out name, he said we needed to take it to the CSU laboratory. "I'm fairly sure they can pull up whatever he wrote. Plus we also now have a sample of his handwriting."

"Right."

When we stopped for a red light, I handed the purloined money order to him. He looked closely at it. "I think I can make out one name here."

"Good. I didn't take time to really look at it. I just stuffed it in my pocket. What do you think it is?"

"It looks like Adam or Aaron or something like that."

"Why don't you call the Feds—"

"You got to be kidding me. Why would I do that?"

"Harry, you've got to get over your prejudices with the Feds. They can run a computer check for someone named Adam or Aaron who owns a motorcycle. We can talk to Motor Vehicles, but the Feds resources go much deeper than ours . . ."

"Good going girl, but we need to be sure on this name, and let's wait and see what our CSU can do first."

"You mean it? You're not just saying it. I thought you didn't—"

"I don't like them, but I never said they couldn't be useful at times. And this is one of those times. Like you say, they have the technology that we don't, and we'd be dumb not to take advantage of their database."

Will wonders never cease, I thought, as Harry parked the car at headquarters and we made our way inside.

"You two need to get upstairs right away," said Cherokee Hack who was working the donut again.

"What's up?" I asked.

"I don't know exactly, but your Commander may be on the carpet with the Assistant Chief," said Cherokee. "*And* some FBI types are up there, too."

"Shit," said Harry. We hurried to the elevator and made our way up to the third floor.

As we approached the Commander's office, Lianne spotted us and waved us inside. "Here's Albright and Barrow now. Do you two have an update for us?" Commander Olivera, the previous head of homicide and now supervising major crimes, and Assistant Chief Shauna Jacobson were sitting in front of Lianne's desk. FBI agents Argent and Reed were standing over to one side. Each of them had grim faces.

Commander Olivera wore a navy suit with a light blue silk tie and a light blue dress shirt. The suit looked good on him with his dark hair and eyes.

Assistant Chief Jacobson wore a charcoal suit with a lilac-colored silk blouse and looked a little like a FBI agent herself.

"As a matter of fact, we came up with some information a few minutes ago," I said. "We came back up here in order to contact Agents Argent and Reed. We can really use their help."

"Whatever you have may be exactly—" Olivera spoke up.

"We need something—" Lianne started.

"You don't know yet because it hasn't been announced, but another woman has been shot," said Commander Olivera.

"Not a policewoman, however," said Lianne. "Although she *was* shot with a rifle. We do think this is a domestic violence case."

Assistant Chief Jacobson said, "But the press is screaming, and it's imperative we have something to give them at the Chief's press conference at three p.m."

Harry and I told them what we had. Everyone got excited, and the FBI agents said just give them that money order and they'd take it from there.

"Okay," said Harry. "But please do us the courtesy of telling us what you find as soon as you find it."

"Will do," said Agent Argent. Harry harrumphed loud enough for both Lianne and Shauna to hear. They both frowned at him, but neither said anything.

"You can tell the press that we have new information," said Lianne to Shauna. "And that we expect a break in the case shortly."

"That will work," said Shauna Jacobson.

"Isn't that a bit premature," I said.

"Yes, but we need to give them something," said Shauna. "We've got to hold them back for now. And who knows? You just got one break, and now we'll hope for another."

The FBI agents said they'd go right now and start working on the marked out ink. They obviously had no interest in a domestic shooting. And they acted like they had our policewoman sniper case under control. Who knows, I thought. Maybe they do.

"You *will* call me immediately," said Lianne.

"Of course. Immediately if not sooner," said Argent.

He and Reed brushed by Harry and I. I couldn't help noticing the smirk on their lips as they looked at Harry.

Harry's fist balled up, but he didn't move.

"What's the story about the new victim?" I asked.

"Esperanza Ramos was parked in her car out in Zilker Park," said Commander Olivera. "A family visiting from

Seattle happened to see her, thought she looked odd, her head at an unusual angle. When the father got closer to check, he dialed 911."

"And she's a civilian," said Shauna. "She'd been shot. No witness or no evidence. Just a random shooting. The only thing similar is she's a Mexican-American female killed by a rifle bullet."

"Jeeze Louise, that makes three women," I said. "What's this guy's agenda anyway?"

"We don't think this one is connected to your case," said Lianne. "She had a restraining order against her ex-husband. We're looking for him."

"Have you got anything else?" asked Lianne.

That's when I realized Assistant Chief Jacobson had made no more comments. Obviously, she was there mainly to observe and report to the Chief.

"Our sniper sicko is somehow getting these girls to get a butterfly tattoo on their left buttocks and then he slices it off?" Olivera's dark eyes held such sadness. "And this tattoo is how you discovered the money order?"

"Yes, sir. We found the tattoo parlor and from there found the mailbox."

"How did you get to see their files without a court order or shouldn't I ask?"

"No, sir," I said. "It's better that you don't know those details."

"Nothing illegal, I hope?" Lianne asked.

"It was entirely legal," Harry said.

"Even though you don't think this one is connected, Lianne," said Olivera. "I'd better contact the Medical Examiner to rule it out. We need to know if Esperanza Ramos has a tattoo," said Olivera. "And see if it's still intact on her body."

APD Mourns Loss of

Commander in Traffic Collision

Austin Police Department Commander Shauna R. Jacobson, 46, and her husband, retired Detective Malcolm "Kurt" Jacobson, 42, died in a motorcycle collision that occurred shortly after 7:00 p.m. on Saturday, December 11, 2004.

The motorcycle driven by Detective Jacobson was traveling eastbound in the 19000 block of West State Highway 71 near Bee Creek in Travis County. The motorcycle struck a guardrail and left the roadway. Detective Jacobson and Commander Jacobson, a passenger, were ejected from the motorcycle. They were both pronounced dead at the scene.

Commander Shauna Jacobson graduated from the Austin Police Department Academy in 1984. She was promoted to detective in 1990 and to sergeant in 1994. In 1997, she was promoted to lieutenant and in 2001 earned the rank of commander. As a commander, she supervised the Centralized Investigations Bureau that includes Homicide, Robbery, Major Traffic Investigations, Sex Crimes and Child Abuse units. She had served as commander over the Northeast Area Command and the Training Academy.

Detective Kurt Jacobson graduated from the Austin Police Department Academy in 1991. He was promoted to detective in 1997. During his career as a detective, he was assigned to Centralized Investigations. He retired from the department in 2002.

The Austin Police Department has lost two members of our family and the entire Department mourns this tragic loss. The Austin Police Department extends its deepest sympathy to the Jacobson family in their time of sorrow.

(Press Release from APD
Public Information Office, Dec. 11, 2004)

Chapter Sixteen

Dammit. He couldn't get to "Sweetthang's" tattoo. Too many people in the park. He should have known better, but she insisted they meet near the rose garden at Zilker. This is totally unacceptable. That's what he got for listening to a slut. What do sluts know?

He started his Yamaha and as soon as he hit Mo-Pac, he opened it up to eighty miles an hour. This baby is capable of a hundred and twenty, and he'd had it up to a hundred easy on an open road.

He enjoyed riding his Yamaha. "One of the few pleasures my stupid parents didn't mess up for me," he thought. Everything he liked had been corrupted by his oh-so-loving parents. His alcoholic parents. But he had finally won out over them. Finally bested them. He never touched alcohol, drugs or nasty women. Wouldn't Elena be proud of her little brother now? Why did she have to leave? He could never understand her in a million years. Running off and leaving him that way. Knowing what would probably happen to him without her there to protect him.

Stupid cars. Stupid people in the cars, talking on cell phones. Wreaking havoc behind them and they are totally oblivious. When is this state going to pass a law outlawing cell phones while driving?

"Watch out, bitch. Get off the damn phone." Oh, good,

and she's got two little kids in there jumping around all over the back. Ought to call and report her for endangering kids. Serve her right if they got taken away from her. Nasty, dirty little urchins.

He'd have to find out which funeral home "Sweetthang" would be taken to. Do I have a clue to her real name? Surely she had told him so he could make the appointment for the tattoo, although she hadn't wanted him to pay for it. He'd have to look in his backup disks.

He needed to get home and check the computer. He needed to get home and get cleaned up. Even the air smells dirty. He pushed the motorcycle up to ninety.

"No tattoo yet. I absolutely must have 'Sweetthang's' tattoo," he yelled into the wind.

In Remembrance:

John Gaines, 50, (November 19, 1913)

Officer John Gaines, the only African-American officer on the Austin police force, was shot by George Booth, a deputy constable, at Sixth Street and Trinity Street on November 19, 1913. Booth, who had been making a disturbance, shot Officer Gaines while Gaines was on the telephone summoning help from the police station. At that time, African-American officers were not allowed to arrest whites. Officer Gaines and his wife, Sarah, were originally from Big Spring, Texas.

Chapter Seventeen

◆ ◆ ◆

Lianne insisted we take some down time.

"Don't you want us to follow up on the latest shooting?" I couldn't believe she was dismissing us.

"No. You two have been working almost nonstop for three days. If you don't get some rest you'll start making mistakes, and we don't need mistakes."

"But—" Harry started.

"Don't argue with me, Harry. Argent and Reed will handle this one if there is a connection . . . which I seriously doubt. They'll work with McDonald and Hall who caught the Zilker Park call in the first place, and they are up to speed on what's going on. And you two can't do much until we get the information back from the FBI anyway."

She could tell we weren't happy about it. "Look," she said. "We're going to catch him. Olivera and I are personally heading up these cases. We've more or less formed a task force. And we're working with the FBI because of their resources. And I promise I'll call you if the FBI gets anything for us." She walked around from her desk and patted Harry's shoulder. "Go get some rest."

"I hate being treated like an old man, Lianne."

"I'm not even thinking about age here, Harry. I'm thinking productivity right now. Tired cops can't deliver the goods, and I'm counting on you two to deliver."

Harry said he'd do whatever was necessary. He walked out heading for his desk.

Lianne turned to me. "Now what's the story on Byron? Is he okay?"

I don't know how she knew about Byron, but she always knew what was going on with her people. A good boss should know what's going on in their crew's lives. If there's a problem, then it can be addressed early on and not after it becomes major. "He's fine," I said. "The nurses who took him from Pecan Groves had their hearts in the right place. They just went about it the wrong way."

"Are the nurses going to be charged with anything?" Lianne walked over to the window and looked out. She tried to act unconcerned, but I knew she cared about Byron's well-being. She just had to act like my supervisor at work . . . not my friend.

"I hope not. I'm not pressing charges, and I don't think the Thielepape's family will either." I brushed back hair that had fallen into my face. "I don't know what the nursing home can or will do. I've called a lawyer pal for the nurses, and I'm hoping things turn out okay."

"Have you found a new place for him?" Lianne asked.

"Not yet. That's something I'll do since I have the afternoon off."

"See, I told you you needed some time off." Lianne smiled.

Harry waited for me at my desk. He said he thought he'd go home, watch a little football, and then get ready for his date with Robbie, the mailbox lady.

"Oh, Harry. Surely you don't have to do that?"

"Don't have to, but I want to. Think this might be a most intriguing woman." He turned and headed down the hall.

As I made the drive down the interstate to Riverside Drive and my apartment, I was surprised to realize that I felt a pang of jealousy. Me, jealous over Harry? Could it be just the fact that I would be having dinner alone tonight when usually Harry and I would have dinner together? Or could it be just because Harry would spend the evening with, in his words, an intriguing woman? Harry was my partner, my friend, my mentor.

Had I ever thought of Harry in any other way? As a lover? Nope. Jason? Yeah, sure, but Harry no. I put the thought out of my mind as I pulled my car into my assigned parking space and went inside.

I played with the cats. Then showered and dressed carefully in my dress boots, a pair of dark green slacks and gold cotton sweater. I grabbed a black leather blazer to put on before talking to administrator-type people. Wanted to look prosperous without looking rich.

I'd talked to a couple of pals who'd recently had to put a parent into a nursing home to see which one they might recommend. Golden Acres came highly touted and it was south of me near Saint Edwards University. I called and the administrator's secretary said he had a thirty-minute time slot open if I could be there in the next few minutes. "I'll be right over."

It only took me fifteen minutes to get to the nursing home's front door. Of course, it would take longer during rush hour, but still a shorter time than to Pecan Grove.

The brick building most likely had been built in the past eight or ten years. The lawn was well kept, and I noticed three or four small concrete patios outside some windows. Each had a small tree and flowers decorating the edges of the patios. The trees had either a humming bird feeder or some other type of bird feeder hanging from them. Those rooms must be for ambulatory people I thought as I parked in the side parking lot.

When I walked inside, I was pleasantly surprised. There was no cleaning or chemical odor and no smell of death or old age. Some nursing homes have the worst odors, even if it's only their cleaning solutions. The offices were off the main hallway with the administrator near the front door. There was a small waiting area, and after I told the secretary who I was, she asked me to be seated.

I barely got comfortable when a man came out, walked up and introduced himself as Ted Baker. "I'm glad to meet you, Mrs. Barrow. I understand you are looking for a new home for your husband." Baker was around five feet ten with thinning gray hair and thick glasses that hid his brown eyes. He wore a chocolate brown suit, a beige shirt and chocolate brown tie. His looks were rather plain chocolate, if you know what I mean. If I saw him out on the street, I'd probably think he was an accountant or an insurance salesman. However, his smile looked genuine, and it reached to his eyes.

"Yes—"

He interrupted me. "Then you've come to the right place. Let me show you around."

"Great, if you have time—" Once again Baker cut me off. What's with this guy? Is he rude or does he just like the sound of his own voice?

"I've heard of your situation from my receptionist. I also know of your husband's condition. Well, Kay Googled your husband's name, Byron Barrow, and printed up a copy for me of his whole story. I don't foresee any problems."

Googled Byron's name? Then I realized that term was computer lingo. Somehow, you went to this web site called Google and you could type in names or places or any information you wanted, and the information would be at your fingertips.

For the tour of the facility, Mr. Baker lost his annoying habit of interrupting. Probably all due to nerves, I thought. The first thing he showed me was the nurse's station and the indoor aviary down one hallway. "Many of our patients love coming here to see the birds," Baker said. "Even the ones you think might not ever respond to people somehow respond to the birds."

The aviary was a large glass enclosed birdcage if you will. I counted eight birds inside—four pairs. There were tree limbs, and soil with plants growing, a small birdbath, and a little stream of water and birdhouses and perches, and everything a bird could need that I could see.

"We have a man who comes monthly and checks on their condition. He's the one who built this aviary in the first place."

"It's wonderful," I said, suitably impressed.

Baker then led me around, showing off the patient rooms, the dining room and kitchen, the activities and crafts center, the library and music room, the TV and game room, and the chapel. He introduced me to nurses and orderlies and therapists and I could tell immediately that he was well liked and people seemed to enjoy working here. It could have been an act, but if so, they all did a good job of covering up any dissension or problems.

By now, I was totally impressed and told Mr. Baker what had happened and how I needed to have my husband transferred right away so as not to lose any benefits on Byron's disability. I'd like to move him here if it's okay. Baker agreed, and I said I'd make arrangements to transfer Byron from Cynthia's house the next day.

"Why don't you have Miss Martin contact me?" said Mr.

Baker. "She sounds as if she's the exact type of employee we like to have here at Golden Acres."

"I'll do that," I said. I filled out the necessary paper work to have Byron admitted and wrote out a check for the first month's fee.

Mr. Baker let me choose from three vacant rooms Golden Acres had available. I picked one on the first floor with a window and a patio. There was a bird feeder in the little bur oak tree. I felt the window presented some visual stimulation for my husband, which the doctors have said, was very important. The room was also near the nurse's station so they could easily check on Byron several times daily and nightly.

With everything set, I shook hands with Mr. Baker and left.

Instead of calling Cynthia, I went over to her house and gave her the news. "Look, I know you wanted to have your own health care center, but—"

"We're still going to do it," she smiled. "Lucy is going to run it. I'll still need to work a full-time job but will be here in the evenings."

"How can you pull double-duty like that?" I asked.

"It will work because we'll have good help. My sister and Lucy's daughter both are qualified if we need them, and I'll only be here and be on call. Not really on duty as it were. And for now, we'll just have Sam T. and Virginia. They're ambulatory . . . well, at least partially, so caring for them won't be too hard."

"So the Thielepapes are staying. I'm glad. I wish I could leave Byron here, but I think since he needs physical therapy and more care than you're equipped for here, that he'll be better off in a larger facility."

"I understand," she said. "When are you moving him?"

"Tomorrow. To Golden Acres and guess what? Mr. Baker the administrator wants you to apply there. He's inclined to put you to work . . . sight unseen."

"Okay. Why don't I take Byron tomorrow myself, and I'll apply for a job while there."

With things underway to having my life settled once again, I headed back to my apartment.

I sure as hell didn't want to eat dinner alone. I called Lianne. She and Kyle, her new husband, were taking his little girl out to eat pizza and then to see a movie. I mentally ran through my list of possible single pals but no one fit my mood.

Melody and Lyric had greeted me happily, with leg rubs and meows of delight, they reminded me that I'm really never alone. I could have dinner with my cat pals and then gird myself for a visit with Levi and Jean Barrow, and discuss moving Byron with them.

That decision made, I hurriedly stripped and dressed in my sloppy, but comfortable sweats and my house shoes. Just as I finished brushing my hair, my front door bell rang. I looked through the peephole and was surprised to see Jason Foxx. I opened the door.

He took one look at me and said, "Zoe? What's going on?"

"Whatever do you mean, Jason?"

"Didn't you agree to have dinner with me last night?"

"Did I? I'm sorry." Oh hell, I had forgotten.

"I waited out in your parking lot for two hours and decided I'd made a mistake and maybe it was tonight we were to meet. I left you a voice mail but didn't hear back."

"I think my cell phone has died." I sat down on the sofa and Jason sat across from me. "I'm really sorry," I said.

"I've been so wrapped up in this case, working from early to late. When I do get home, most of the time, all I want to do is get a shower and fall into bed."

"You're home *early* tonight?"

"Well, I suddenly had the evening off, and I really am sorry I forgot."

"Have you eaten?" Jason asked.

"No, have you?"

"No, so let's go somewhere. How about bar-b-que?"

"Sounds good, Jason." I looked closely at him. He was wearing brushed denim jeans and a green and black and white striped shirt. He looked exceptionally good. And my sloppy attire was suited for home but not to go out someplace. "Let me change and refresh my make-up," I said.

"You look great," he said. "In fact, if it weren't for the dark circles under your eyes, I'd say you're looking better than usual."

"Gosh, Jase, you really know how to flatter a girl. Makes my heart go pitty-pat."

He laughed. "One of my specialities."

"I'm sure you'll clue me in on all the others." I left him sitting on the sofa trying to coax Melody up on his lap and hurried to the bedroom to change into Levi's and a cotton knit top.

After we'd gotten settled at the restaurant and our food had arrived, Jason asked, "Things getting rather dicey around APD aren't they?"

"It's been grim." I told him a little . . . I couldn't give too many details since he's a civilian. "And Harry hates sharing with the FBI." We were stuffing ourselves with brisket and sausage and chicken, and trying to talk at the same time. Not easy, I can attest to.

Jason laughed. "Oh, yeah, knowing Harry, I can imagine how he's handling the Feds."

"He calls them Feebs. It's like he sees them as against us or something. He doesn't want to share information with them, and yet he wants every scrap of info they turn up."

Jason shook his head. "Most cops his age had bad experiences with the Feds somewhere along the line and now are so distrustful."

"How about you?" I asked. "Did you have trouble with them?" I had never really learned too much about his career as a cop in Houston. I knew he'd been shot and either had to leave the force or just couldn't take the stress anymore. A number of officers leave after being shot. Too much like tempting fate.

"Not me. I got along famously with them, but I also took some training at Quantico and have great respect for most of those guys." He finished chewing, wiped his mouth, and asked if I wanted dessert.

"Ohh, nooo. I'm much too full. I would like some more iced tea if we can catch our waitress."

Jason ordered the tea for me and a beer for himself and then asked, "What else is on your mind, Zoe? I know the case is eating at you, but something else is wrong."

"You really are perceptive, Jason. I have been very worried about Byron, but things are working out."

"What's wrong? Is he sick?"

I told him the story of the kidnapping and how I'd finally located my husband and how he'd be transferred to the new nursing home tomorrow.

"So, Cynthia was just worried that Byron was in danger?"

"Yes," I said. "And I believe she was right in her feelings. The new owners are only about making money."

"Can you get them investigated?" Jason asked.

"Yes, I've already reported them and the state is going to investigate."

I was tired and told Jason we needed to call it an evening. I wanted to keep this dinner on a friendship basis, and I insisted on paying my portion of the check.

Jason didn't protest and drove me home. Once inside, he put his arms around me, thanked me for a nice evening and held me close.

I wanted to respond. I could feel myself wanting the comfort he was offering. Not just sex, but a connection with someone who I felt cared for me. As I started to pull away, he kissed me. I could feel the tingle run down my spine all the way to my toes.

Get hold of yourself, Zoe, I thought. You're not ready for this, I told myself. I pulled away gently. "Sorry, Jase."

"I understand, Zoe," he said. "I just want you to know I'm here if you need a friend or a shoulder or even if you ever need more than a friend." He walked to my door and closed it softly behind him.

I was relieved, but also felt a lot more alone as he left. Alone and lonely and cold.

The message light on my answering machine was blinking. I pressed the "play" button. Levi Barrow's voice boomed out. My father-in-law sounded more than a little agitated. "What's this about you moving Byron out of Pecan Groves? And where is he anyway?"

Hoo-boy, I sure was too tired to deal with the Barrows tonight. I'll call them tomorrow.

I slipped into my big nightshirt and headed for bed. I know I dreamed of Jason and Byron, but when the alarm went off, I couldn't remember exactly what the dream had been about.

The next morning, I called Harry and said I'd be late. That Byron was being moved today. I made myself a good breakfast of waffles and sausage and ate out on deck. Lyric came outside, but as usual, Melody stayed sitting in the patio doorway and watched. Lyric chased a moth that was somnolent in the daylight and after he caught it, he ate it. I thought it was yucky, but Lyric licked his chops for ten minutes, so I guess he enjoyed it.

I called Levi Barrow and left a message that Byron was moving to Golden Acres Nursing and Retirement Center today, and I'd talk to them later.

I drove to Golden Acres and found Cynthia had already moved Byron in and had him settled. Byron was resting easy when I walked into his room. I brushed his hair and checked to see if his nails needed cutting. They didn't. Cynthia came in a few minutes later. "Mrs. Barrow?"

"Hey, Cynthia. You know you can call me Zoe."

"I know."

"You've already started to work here?" I asked.

"Yes. They hired me on the spot and wanted me to start this morning. I appreciate you talking to them in my be-half."

"No problem. I know what a great nurse you are and I was happy to do it."

"Thanks," she said. "I really do appreciate it."

Suddenly she looked as if a wave of nausea had hit her stomach. "I need to talk to you about something, and I'm really nervous about it." A worried frown creased Cynthia's light brown face.

"What's wrong, Cynthia? You can tell me."

"I know. Let's go down the hall to the craft room and

talk. There's no one in there right now, and I don't think we'll be interrupted."

"Okay," I said and followed her down the hall.

After we were seated, she looked at me for a few seconds, then said, "I've known you for almost two years now, and I think you're a very kind and caring person. And I know you're also a very smart lady."

"Thank you, Cynthia. And I have complete faith in your nursing abilities. You've proved that for years taking such good care of Byron. Besides, I count you as a friend to both Byron and myself."

"Which is why I need to tell you all about this. Mr. Barrow's parents came here this morning and they's unhappy 'cause you moved Byron away from Pecan Grove."

I had left a message only an hour or so ago. How had they managed to hear that and gotten over here so quickly, I wondered. Must have come over as soon as they heard what I'd said. Strange, I decided. Very strange.

"Well, they don't have any say in that decision. Byron is my husband, and I'm in charge of his medical decisions."

"I think it was mostly Mr. Byron's mother who was complaining. After talking to me, she talked at length with our administrator, Mr. Baker. I think she's wanting to get me fired."

"I wouldn't worry. Jean Barrow is all bluster. Her husband Levi is reasonable, and he usually keeps her under control. And I'm not going to let her do anything to cause you any problems."

She smiled in relief, but I could tell she was still struggling with something in her mind. I saw it in her eyes when she made the decision to tell me all.

"Maybe I shouldn't tell, but I think you should know."

Man, I absolutely didn't like the sound of that.

In Remembrance:

Drew Alan Bolin, 25, (June 2, 1995)
Officer Drew Bolin was killed in the line of duty when he was struck by a drunk driver while directing traffic at a collision site in the 4800 block of IH-35. The driver of the vehicle, Cessilee Hyde, was convicted of intoxication manslaughter. Officer Bolin was in his fifth month of service as a commissioned officer of the Austin Police Department at the time of his death.

(Austin City Connection -
The Official Web site of the City of Austin)

Chapter Eighteen

◆　◆　◆

As soon as I got to headquarters, I knew something bad had happened. Detective Donald Romero was working the front desk, and one look at his face was a giveaway. "What's wrong? What's happened?" I asked.

Don was a good friend. He'd gone to the academy with Byron. He was late-forties, hazel eyes, shaved head and muscles to spare. He looked great in his patrol blues. Normally he worked plain clothes in Narcotics, but for the front desk, he wore the APD uniform. "You'd better get upstairs and fast," Donald said. "Albright's been trying to call your cell phone."

I had just got a new phone, my old one had died. I had the same phone number. Why couldn't he reach me? As I swiped my ID card into the elevator card box, I checked my phone. "Damn." I'd forgotten to turn on the phone.

I hurried down the hall to my cubicle to find Harry looking worse than I'd ever seen him. He looked unshaven and disheveled, and I realized he was wearing the same clothes as he'd worn yesterday. "Harry? Sorry, I had to turn my phone off for a little while, and I forgot to turn it back on. What's up?"

"Sit down," and his voice broke. "Dammit it. This is not easy."

I sat, and knew it was real bad.

"Anne Panzarella was shot this morning—she's alive, but barely. They're doing surgery now."

"Oh, dear God, no. Not Anne. Was she shot? By our sniper?"

"She was shot, but they don't think it was by our sniper guy."

"What happened?" I couldn't help the tears.

"They're not exactly sure. They found her in a squad car in Edward sector about five thirty this morning," he said and his voice cracked as he spoke. "One bullet was a grazing shot to her face that took off part of her ear and a groove across her cheek and face. The other more serious shot to her left shoulder and chest area. She lost a lot of blood because she sat there for some time before she was found."

"What was she doing out there and at that time of the morning?'

"Not sure. It's still under investigation."

"Oh, man. Are we going to get involved?" I asked.

"Not really. We've got our own case to work, and I think they need us to focus on our sniper."

"Damn. Man, I just can't believe it. We just had lunch last week while I was doing my role-plays days out at the academy. We were together the day Sanchez got shot."

"I know. And I've known Anne for years. She was a damn good cop." He choked up a bit. "I know Paul, her husband, and I've been around her kids so much they call me Uncle Harry."

"This is so unreal," I said. "It just can't be true. We're sure it's Anne?"

"Yes, I went out there this morning. I didn't shave or anything. I just jumped into what I'd worn last night and hauled ass out there."

"And we still don't know what happened?"

Lianne Crowder walked up. "I want you two to drop the sniper case and focus on who shot Anne."

"Are you sure? We're getting close to this sniper," Harry said. "As much as I'd like to work on Anne's shooting—"

"Look, Harry. This came from upstairs. The brass wants you on this because you're the best. The Feds have developed a couple of leads from the receipt you gave them so they'll continue with the sniper case."

"Man, I knew those guys would screw us, didn't I tell you, Zoe?"

"Harry," said Lianne. "The FBI hasn't got to you. They're working on information you provided. The brass and I . . . everyone . . . wants you on Anne's case. If anyone can find out what happened, you can. You're the best investigator I've got. And I want the best right now."

"And you want me working with Harry?" I asked.

"Yes, he needs someone to help keep him in line on this," said Lianne. "We don't want him going off half-cocked. Normally, we might not put him into the investigation, but like I said, Harry is the best investigator we got right now. And we know we can depend on you." She turned to me. "And Zoe, I know I can depend on you when Harry gets . . ."

"Okay, okay," said Harry. "I get the picture."

"And I've got mine," I said.

"Okay, then let's get busy," Harry said. "Here's my notes and sketches from this morning Zoe. CSU is probably still working the scene. Let's get out there."

"Who is out there, Lianne?" I knew homicide wouldn't leave the scene.

"Olivera. He's expecting you both."

Boy, was I relieved. I sure didn't want to step on anyone's toes over this one, and since Olivera was a supervisor himself, he wouldn't be upset.

Harry and I headed outside. He beat me to the driver's side. But since we needed to get to the location quickly, I didn't really mind. There were thunderstorms building in the southwest, dark billowing clouds and lightening strikes jagging their way to the ground, but we scarcely noticed. Our minds were filled with the horrors of what had happened to our friend and colleague, Anne.

A large abandoned building that had once been a grocery store with a large parking lot was the crime scene. Five squad cars, a CSU vehicle and a fire truck were parked haphazardly near the police vehicle where Anne had been found. Commander Olivera was talking to the CSU technicians we worked with earlier, Massey and Greyson.

"Glad to see you Harry," said Olivera. "And you too, Zoe. Commander Crowder informed me earlier that the two of you would be primary here." He paused and looked at the CSU technicians. "You know everyone?"

"Yes, sir," said Massey. "I've worked with Albright many times, and we both worked with he and Mrs. Barrow just the other day out at Mansfield Dam."

"Of course, on the second sniper shooting."

"What you found so far?" Harry asked Massey.

Greyson went back over to the vehicle to continue processing.

"Looks as if Sergeant Panzarella was shot at point blank range," Massey said. "We'll know more when we process her clothing. The EMS people said they'd send her things over to the lab. Have you heard how she is doing?"

"Lianne said Anne was still in surgery before we left headquarters," I said. I knew in a few minutes Harry and I would be checking the car, and I knew how hard that was going to be just knowing that it was Anne's blood all over the seat.

"Lianne called here just before you two arrived to tell me you were on the way," Olivera said. "And she said Anne was just now in recovery. It's going to be touch and go for the next twenty-four, forty-eight hours. I'll leave it with you, Albright." Olivera hitched up his slacks and headed to his marked command vehicle.

"We'd better get busy," said Harry.

"Car's been wiped clean of prints," said Greyson.

"We're going to vacuum and bag everything right now," Massey said.

"Let me know when you've finished," said Harry. "I'll call the wrecker to haul it to our secure impound lot."

"Will do," said Massey.

A couple of patrol officers had been keeping back the small crowd of onlookers. I walked over to speak with the officers while Harry continued with the technicians. One of the police officers stepped forward to meet me.

"Mrs. Barrow? I'm Eric Davey. I knew your husband before he went to SWAT, but don't think I ever met you." He extended his hand. He stood about five feet eleven, with a crew cut, dark hair, and a small cut on his chin where he'd cut himself shaving this morning. "How is Byron?"

"Glad to meet you, Eric. Byron's about the same. No real change. Thanks for asking."

"Real shame, Ma'am."

"Thank you," I cleared my throat. "Now to the business at hand. Did anyone see anything or hear anything?"

"Naw, these are all looky-loos."

The other officer walked up. "Jack Pugh," he said, offering his hand.

Pugh was another of those tall, blonde surfer-looking

guys we sometimes get from California. However, his accent was pure Texan. "Do you want us to start a canvas? The only housing I see is that apartment building over there." He pointed catty-corner across the street.

"I'll go with you, Eric, and Jack, if you will, stay with Albright and see what he wants to do," I said.

"Sure." Pugh walked back and spoke to Harry. Harry looked at me and waved us on.

Officer Davey and I knocked on every door in the apartment building. If someone was at home, they didn't see or hear anything. Or if they did, they were not talking to the cops. We were about to give up when we came to the last apartment on the far corner.

Eric Davey knocked. A wizened little black man answered. His face was as wrinkled as an unironed shirt, and he was bent over from the waist with a severe curvature of the spine. We introduced ourselves and said we were investigating the shooting that had happened outside and could we talk with him for a minute?

He looked at our identification badges and then opened the door for us to enter. He said his name was Carl Locke, he was eighty-seven-years old, and he lived alone. His eyes were red-rimmed and watery, but I think because of allergies or a cold. He invited us in.

We walked inside and were almost stifled by the heat. "I's sorry about the heat, but it seems like I's cold just all the time. Guess it's this medicine I's takin' to thin my blood."

"It's fine, Mr. Locke," I assured him. He and I sat down on the sofa and Officer Davey stood nearby. "We're investigating that police officer getting shot over there across the street. Did you see or hear anything that might help us?"

"Yessum, well, I's up and down all night, Ma'am. I gots

postate trouble, excuse me for talking so plain, Ma'am."

"That's all right, Mr. Locke. Did you see or hear anything when you got up?"

"I got up 'bout four o'clock and I wanted me a drink of milk. So I went to the kitchen and poured me a glass of milk. I was sitting there drinking it and I heard a motorsickle making a loud noise."

Motorcycle, I thought. Could it be possible it was the same one our sniper drove? Could our sniper have changed his method and decided to get up close and personal this time? Was he getting even more careless?

"I looked out my window and I saw this black and silver motorsickle and it took off thataway." He pointed southward.

"Did you get a look at the driver?"

"No, ma'am. He had one of them helmets . . . it were like that Darth Vader guy from that movie. I's don't go to no movies but I sees things on TV. On Halloween some of the lil' kids around here dress like that there Darth Vader."

Despite his age and infirmities, Mr. Locke seemed to know what he was talking about. He didn't talk or act senile in any way. I suggested to Officer Davey that he go over to ask Harry Albright to come over here to hear this story.

When Harry came by, he listened attentively as Mr. Locke went through his story again and was as impressed as I by the man's mental recall. We asked Mr. Locke if he would go downtown with Officer Davey and Officer Pugh and give an official statement to headquarters.

"Yessum, I be glad to."

Harry and I went back outside, and in a few moments, Officer Davey and Mr. Locke climbed into the patrolmen's squad car. I noticed Officer Pugh had gotten into the back "prisoner section," allowing Mr. Locke to ride up front with Eric Davey.

"What do you make of all this, Harry? You think our sniper did this and is taunting us by using a handgun instead of a rifle?"

"Not so much what I think, Zoe, but what it seems the evidence is taking us."

"Yeah, guess we don't want to jump to conclusions. It just strikes me as odd. This is the fourth woman shot within a week. Two were Mexican-American policewomen; one was Hispanic, but not a policewoman. And now Anne, a policewoman, but not Hispanic."

"Three shot with a rifle," Harry said. "A motorcycle found near or reported near three. Do we have anything yet on the Zilker Park shooting?"

"I'll check with Lianne and get an update," I said.

We finished up the scene and headed back to headquarters. We got the latest information from the FBI guys and on the Zilker Park shooting and discovered Esperanza Ramos had been a police officer in San Antonio.

Lianne came in from the hospital to report on Anne. "She's holding on, but that's all anyone can say."

"I'm going over to see how her family's doing," Harry said.

"I'll go over, too, but I can't stay. I've got to meet with Byron's parents."

"Good luck," said Harry. "Call me later."

"I may have to call you to come bail me out."

When I got to my car, I pulled out my cell phone and called Levi and Jean's house. I could only feel relief when Levi answered the phone. I wasn't ready to talk to Jean just yet.

"How are you, Zoe?"

"Fine, except for a bit of confusion about what you and Jean have been up to at the nursing home. Discussing Byron's treatment behind my back."

"Zoe, none of this is my idea."

"I know that. I know, but you allow Jean to—"

"I don't think we should discuss this over the phone," he said.

"I agree."

"When can you come out here?"

"How about now?"

Levi only hesitated a moment. "Now is fine for me, but I don't know if Jean—"

I didn't much care if Jean wanted to talk to me right now or not. I was ready to talk to her and the sooner the better. "I'll be there in a half-hour."

I couldn't help the knot of apprehension as I made the drive to the Barrow's lovely home in West Lake Hills. Levi Barrow had retired from a real estate and development company, invested wisely in several dot-com companies and moved up to the high-priced area about a year ago.

From the street, the Barrows' Georgian colonial home looked like a mansion. I drove into the circular drive and parked under the portico. The lush lawn was immaculate and looked like a putting green. Late summer roses were still blooming in Jean's side garden, permeating the air with their lovely scent.

Levi opened the front door before I could ring the bell and gave me a hug as I entered the foyer. "Things will be okay, Zoe." His voice was husky.

Looking at the man who had fathered my husband, I felt my throat tighten. It was like looking at Byron if you took away the gray streaks in his dark hair and airbrushed out the wrinkles from around his blue-green eyes. He was dressed in dark blue Levi's and a red plaid western-style shirt.

"I hope so, Levi. I really hope so," I told him.

We made our way past the formal living room and dining room and on into the family room where Jean Barrow sat on a cream-colored leather sofa.

"Hello, Jean," I said.

She gave me a smile that didn't quite reach her eyes. Jean had aged in the two years since Byron's accident and with half a kind word from her, I probably would have felt sorry for her. "Zoe," was all she said.

Her dark hair was highlighted to cover the gray and coiffed to perfection by the very expensive stylist I knew she saw twice a week. Tonight she was dressed in a pale pink silk blouse with dark gray slacks. Diamonds twinkled on her fingers and from her tennis bracelet, and small gold rings were in her ears.

I sat down in the armchair by the fireplace. It was too warm tonight for a fire, but I'd spent a few evenings there with my husband when it was cold, and we'd always enjoyed the fire and the warmth of this room. The memories were bittersweet and, for a moment, the room seemed cold despite the warm weather.

"Jean." I looked over at Levi who stood next to the fireplace, at a distance roughly between Jean and myself. I thought he was making a point of remaining neutral. "Jean, I am at a loss as to why you didn't talk first to me about any medical treatment for *my* husband. I've thought all along that the three of us would always do what was best for Byron."

She looked at Levi, but his face was closed. "We thought you would discuss everything with us, too. Yet you moved *our* son to a new nursing facility without even telling us about it."

"I didn't move him, Jean. Cynthia Martin, the nurse from Pecan Grove moved him and several other patients without my knowledge."

Her voice rose as she began accusing. "That's another thing. You allowed him—"

I couldn't help responding with a louder voice also. "Allowed him? This was all done without me even know—"

"That's right. You didn't even know about—"

"How could I know? Byron's nurse, Cynthia, did it behind my back." How could this woman be so obtuse?

"You should have been taking better—"

"Wait a minute. Just a darn minute. I can't be with Byron every minute of the day. I have to work in order to pay my rent and buy food and anything extra that Byron needs."

"You wouldn't have to work if you'd let us—"

"Don't you realize I'd go bonkers if I didn't work!" No way did I want to be beholden to my in-laws.

Levi finally got into it but with a calming voice and attitude. "Okay, Jean. Okay, Zoe. Let's not get into a quarrel here. Dear, I don't think Zoe could have done anything to prevent the nurses from taking Byron out of Pecan Grove."

"Besides which," I said, "his nurse cares about Byron, and she moved him because she felt he would not receive the best care with the policies of the new management at Pecan Grove. He wasn't harmed in any way. In fact, now he's in an even better place and his favorite nurse, Cynthia, is working there and taking care of him."

Jean sniffed and said, "Maybe that makes it all right." Her tone went from shrill to calm almost as quickly as the lead could change in a Lady Longhorns basketball game.

If she could calm herself so quickly, then so could I. "Okay, that's settled. Now why don't you tell me about this

Swedish doctor and what he thinks the chances are for Byron?"

After her initial surprise that I knew about this doctor, she quickly sketched in how she'd heard of a Doctor Hendrickson in Sweden and how she'd written to him, sending copies of all of Byron's medical records. "He thinks there is a strong possibility he can help Byron with his new technique. But he wants to examine Byron and run some tests on his own."

"So will Doctor Hendrickson come over here?"

"He's going to try to work out his schedule so he can come to America. He needs us to pay his way. We know it would be a hardship on you, but we could afford to do it."

"We were waiting until we knew for sure he thought he could help," said Levi.

"That sounds really good to me. And I have some money saved. I'd be happy to pay his fee. But what I can't understand is why you didn't discuss all this with me before discussing it with the administration at the nursing center."

Jean looked at Levi. I saw some strange look pass between them and then Levi spoke. "I don't agree with Jean about this."

Jean looked at me with what can only be described as hatred. "Zoe, I don't think you want Byron to get better. You have the best of both worlds. You can go out with . . . with any man and have a good time. Yet you'll still have everyone's sympathy no matter what you do. Because your poor husband is in a coma."

I was shocked first and angry next. How dare this woman. Then I looked at Levi. His face showed the same shock and anger I felt. It wasn't easy to do so, but I let my anger cool. I wanted to call her every name in the book, but I didn't. Somehow, I think Levi realized the only reason I

181

held back was because of my love for Byron and for the good feelings I had for Levi.

I stood and looked down at her. I was still angry, but cold and controlled words were what were necessary. "You know, I'd feel sorry for you if you weren't so pathetic. You never thought I was good enough for your son because you're a totally selfish woman. You wanted him to marry some society gal because that might enhance your society standing. You didn't care if he found love as long as you could hobnob with some idea of the Joneses." My animosity for this woman had been years in the making. It was difficult not to scream.

"You never could stand it because Byron and I loved each other and were actually happy. I shouldn't have to tell you this—if you had any sense at all, you'd know that I still love my husband. I don't go out with men. And just to set the record straight—I'd give my right arm to have Byron well and back in my life and back in my arms."

I turned and walked quickly out of their house. It would be a cold day in hell before I'd ever go back again. Tomorrow, I'll get that full guardianship of Byron. She will *never* have a legal leg to stand on and would *never* have any say over any of my husband's medical treatment.

I was furious at both of them. Levi sometimes let Jean have her way instead of standing up to her and telling her when she was wrong. This time he needed to stand up to her. This time she was more than wrong. In my opinion, she was totally bonkers. And as much as I cared for my father-in-law, he was spineless at times. And tonight I lost a great deal of respect for him.

By the time I got home I'd calmed down enough to realize I'd have to contact Levi to find out how to get in touch with Dr. Hendrickson and see if the man could come to

Austin. If there was any possibility to help Byron, I definitely wanted it done. No matter what it cost. But I'd discuss it with Levi, not with Jean. I meant it when I said she will never have any say in Byron's care if I have anything to do with it.

In Remembrance:

Clinton Warren Hunter, 22, (November 29, 2001)
Officer Clinton Hunter died from fatal injuries sustained when a vehicle, driven by a suspect attempting to flee from patrol officers, struck him. Officer Hunter was in his 14th month of service as a commissioned officer of the Austin Police Department at the time of his death. The suspect, Herschel Hinkle, eventually pleaded guilty of intoxication manslaughter and was sentenced to life in prison.

(Austin City Connection -
The Official Web site of the City of Austin)

Chapter Nineteen

My phone was ringing as I walked into my apartment. It was Harry.

"How did it go with the Barrows? Get things straightened out?"

"Oh, yeah . . . *NOT!* You ain't gonna believe this." When I finished telling him, he told me it was hard to understand a woman like that.

"You can't let her get you down," he said. "Do you want me to come over and confiscate your weapon?"

"Take my gun, why?"

"So you won't be tempted to go over and shoot her."

I burst out laughing and felt better immediately. "I think I can control myself, but if I start feeling the urge to kill, I'll call you, okay?"

"It's a deal. Now let me tell you my good news. The Feebs have identified a suspect through the motorcycle registration. A scumbag named Warren Adams."

"How sure are they that this is our sniper?"

"About ninety-five percent right now. Actually, they were able to find out from the letters W-AD-MS from that mailbox receipt, it spelled out WARREN ADAMS. They crosschecked that with Yamaha motorcycle registrations and licensing. But we need to come up with some hard evidence. The Feebs are going to stake out his house. If he even farts, they'll know it."

"And we can get hard evidence how?"

"Our good luck is Warren has a rap sheet for suspicion of arson, but not convicted. He's been photographed and fingerprinted. He has a juvie record that was sealed, and the Feds are trying to get that open to see what help that might be. We'll take a photo lineup to the tattoo parlor and see if Annie Frannie can identify him. The same with the mailbox lady, Robbie."

"By the way, how did your evening with Robbie go?"

"We had a good time. She's a nice lady, but she's not really my type."

"Whatever your type is," I said.

"*I want a gir-ul just like the gir-ul—*" he sang off-key.

"Please. Have mercy on my ears."

He laughed. "Okay, back to cases. We need to talk to CSU about that palm print from the fire cadets' tower and see if it matches."

"Right. I'm betting it does match," I said.

"Look, I'm giving you an order," said Harry. And Harry never gave orders. "Go home, and get some rest tonight, and we'll jump back into investigating Anne's shooting first thing tomorrow."

Harry picked me up shortly after seven, offering mocha cappuccino and Krispy Kremes to appease me for getting me up so early. He knows I'm never too thrilled to ride with him. Harry's driving sometimes scares me so much that I swear I get three more gray hairs every time I ride with him. He drives defensively but fast.

"Think this will work?" He handed me a photo array. He'd done an excellent job choosing photos of males who looked similar to this Warren Adams . . . hair color, eye color, size. He had eight pics, three of them were police officers and the remainders were bad guys.

"Looks good, but what about our other assignment to Anne's case?" I asked.

"Nothing says we can't do both, right? We're very talented that way," he said.

We made it to Annie Frannie's just as she was opening her tattoo parlor. Who wanted to get a tattoo at eight in the a.m.? I wondered. She didn't look too happy to see us, but she agreed to look at the photos.

"I don't know what this guy looked like," Annie Frannie said. "He never came with the girls, and he always paid by invoice like I told you before."

"It won't hurt you to take a look and see if anyone looks familiar," Harry said.

She took the photos but reluctantly.

"Look closely," I said. "It's important."

I could see she was actually doing as I asked, not just scanning. "You'll be not only doing us a favor," I said, "but yourself too, because Harry and I will both remember how you helped. And it's nice to have a couple of cops owing you." I laughed a little as if to say that was a little joke, but that she might call us for some minor help.

"Hey!" She pointed to Warren Adams. "This guy's been in twice. God, I remember him, although it's been about two or three years. I honestly don't know if he's the one who's been sending the girls in here. But the last time he was in here, we had a funny conversation."

"Funny how?" I asked.

Annie Frannie said, "Just—"

"Funny weird or funny haha?" I interrupted.

"Ohh. Funny weird." Her eyes got bigger and bigger as she remembered. "He asked me a lot about butterflies. Said his sister always loved butterflies. That she was dead now, but that I had put a butterfly tattoo on her about four or five years earlier."

Harry looked at me but didn't say anything. I knew he wanted me to follow up on that remark. I had to be careful not to lead her to what we wanted her to say.

"So you had tattooed his sister?"

"Yeah. I didn't really remember her until he kept talking about her. Said she was the most beautiful girl he's ever seen. Long dark hair, dark eyes and olive skin.

"So I asked him, you mean I gave her a butterfly tattoo? And he said, oh yes. On her left buttocks. And how surprised he was when he saw it."

"He saw this tattoo on his sister's butt?"

"Yeah, that's what was weird. His sister was older, he said, and was his adopted sister. I had a feeling she was maybe six or eight years older. And I couldn't help wondering why was she showing her butt to her younger brother even if she was an adopted sister and not blood-related. Perverted family sounded to me like."

I nodded. "Maybe he snuck around and peeked when she was bathing or changing clothes. Something like that. Did he say why he was so surprised to see the butterfly tattoo?" I asked.

Annie Frannie grinned. "Said he just didn't know her brown skin went all the way down to her butt and below."

"That does sound like a sneaky little brother rather than a perversion."

"Yeah, well. I guess. But there's one more weird thing."

"What else?" Harry spoke up for the first time.

"While I was talking to him, I finally remembered his sister being here."

"You remembered someone who's been in your shop—

what?—at that time maybe five years earlier?" I couldn't keep the incredulous tone from my voice.

"Yes, but it was only because he was telling me so much about her. And because that's when I designed that exact tattoo. It was an Atlides Halesus."

"A what?" Harry and I spoke in unison.

"Great Purple Hairstreak. This butterfly is all black and blue, a real beauty. And while I was inking it on her, I remembered this girl telling me she was a cop in Houston. Look, I've put that Blue Hairstreak on hundreds of gals in the past seven or eight years, but she was the first and I've never forgotten her. Beautiful young Hispanic woman."

We thanked Annie Frannie and headed over to Speedway to talk to Harry's mailbox lady.

"His sister's a cop—" Harry said.

"A butterfly tattoo on Mexican-American women."

"He's got a hard-on for female cops or just ones who look like his sister?" Harry asked, not expecting an answer.

"He snuck around and saw her nude? Or did she molest him? That might explain his hate of female Hispanic cops," I said.

"We're on this guy's tail," said Harry. "And," he beat on the steering wheel, "I want this freaking A-hole."

"We'll get him, Harry."

My cell phone rang. Commander Crowder's voice sounded tense and abrupt. "Where are you two right now?"

"On Speedway," I said. "We're on our way to talk to Robbie Serpico at the mail-box store. We got some righteous information from Annie Frannie. And we want Ms. Serpico to collaborate."

"That's good, but let's skip the mail-box lady for now. Get back up here ASAP."

"Right," I said to Lianne. Then I told Harry to turn

189

around and head back to headquarters.

He made a left turn and headed for Loop 1. "Did Lianne say how Anne Panzarella was doing?" Harry asked.

"No." We went under an overpass, and I thought I'd lost the cell signal. In fact, I sort of hoped I had lost her. I didn't know what I'd say if she asked why we were still working on the sniper case. In about thirty seconds, I realized the cell phone connection was still open as I could hear her talking to someone in the background. And fortunately, she didn't ask why we were doing what we were doing. "Lianne? You still there? How is Anne?"

"The Feds came up with an address for Adams," Lianne said. "We're getting a warrant, and they want to hit it now."

"Okay," I said. I heard more noise in the background.

"Hold on a minute," Lianne said. When she came back to me, she said, "Argent and Reed are heading to the address now. You're to meet them there. They've got a warrant."

Lianne was silent for a moment. "Uh, Anne is still critical, but she is a little better, and they think she'll pull through, but it still can go either way."

"Okay, sounds good," I said. I told Harry what the Feds were going to do and that we needed to head that way, too.

"Why am I not surprised at those clowns. The Feebs want to steal the collar," said Harry.

Lianne overheard him. "Dammit, Harry . . . we don't really care as long as we get this cop killer off the street, now do we?" Lianne's voice was firm.

"We agree, Lianne. Give us the address," I said.

Harry hit the access ramp and entered Loop 1, also known as Mo-Pac to the locals because the Missouri-Pacific Railroad originally had the right away, and even today a portion of the railroad tracks still run down the center of the freeway. In fact, we were currently catching up to a freight train as we headed south. Seeing that train in the middle of the highway was a bit strange. But I guess that's not any stranger than a railroad crossing across the middle of Interstate Highway 35. All part of what keeps Austin weird.

We followed Mo-Pac to its end and took Highway 71 west at the "Y" in Oak Hill. We followed along for a few miles, then turned south onto a winding asphalt Ranch Road.

Not really a neighborhood but several houses along the way. Many nice trees, pecan, ash, magnolia and live oak, and far enough from town that most had some acreage. A few houses had dying vegetable gardens—too late in the season—and many others had horses, cows, and goats in small pastures. The farther along we went, the sparser the houses. I was hoping we were on the right road.

As we rounded a curve, we spotted a dark sedan ahead that definitely looked like government issue. Harry pulled over onto the grassy berm, we parked and got out. Everything was quiet . . . too quiet. No birds chirping, no farm animals braying or mooing or whatever they did. We moved slowly closer to the neat white house. The house had tall grass and weeds and a few dying flowers in a flower bed.

Harry pulled out his weapon, and I got my Glock out of my fanny pack and strung my police ID around my neck.

Suddenly we spotted Craig Reed as he half-crawled and hobbled through the grass and dirt trying to reach us. "Am . . . bu . . . lance. Offi . . . cer down."

Harry grabbed Reed. "Where's Argent? Where's the shooter?"

Reed pointed towards the back of the house. His right leg was covered in blood and so was his right shoulder. "Shooter got away." He surprised us both by passing out. Harry eased him to the ground.

"Don't think he's hurt too bad. He's probably just fainted," said Harry. "Let's check this place out. Use your walkie-talkie and call communications. Then let's see if we can find Argent. Maybe he's still alive."

I called the communications supervisor and she said she'd get EMS on the way. And all the other personnel we needed—more officers, CSU technicians, supervisors and the commander on duty.

Harry headed to the front door and told me to take the back. As I rounded the corner of the house and took a quick peek down the side, I thought I heard a motor receding in the woods behind the house.

Then I could hear Harry over my walkie-talkie directing the ambulance, the supervisor and backup. "Zoe, watch your step," he said to me.

"Okay, you too," I said. "Hey, I thought I heard a motorcycle off in the distance a minute ago."

"Hold on, Zoe. Reed's trying to tell me something. I'll get back to you."

"Adams left," I heard Reed's voice through Harry's radio. "Shot Lon and me. I think Lon's dead. Adams left on a motorbike. He was in that barn in back when he opened up on us."

"I think I heard the motorcycle a minute ago," I told Harry again.

"Wonder what spooked him?" Harry asked. He sounded quite disappointed, and I knew it was because he desperately wanted to get Adams.

"Can we get the police helicopter in the air?"

Harry said he'd call in and request the chopper. "I'm sure Commander Crowder will okay it."

"Anyone else around?" I asked Harry. The answer came from Reed. "Not sure. Don't think so."

Then Harry spoke again. "Sounds like Reed's passed out again. See if you can find Argent."

I eased around to the back side of the house and saw a man laying in the grass near the back door. I walked over slowly, doing my best to make sure no one was lurking nearby. No doubt about it being Argent. A pool of blood was spreading around him, and as I bent down to check for a pulse, I knew it was hopeless. The left side of his head was gone. It wasn't pretty. I felt my stomach tighten, but I kept my gag reflex under control.

"Awww, Lonnie. What happened?" I didn't know this FBI agent very well, and I thought he was too cocky for his own good, but I didn't want him dead. "If you had just waited on us. Like Harry said, you guys just wanted the collar yourself. You just had to be hot dogs and show up APD. Damn you." I felt tears welling up and spilling over.

I didn't know for sure what had gone down, but the one thing I was absolutely sure of now . . . Adams had just signed his death warrant ten times over. Killing APD female officers put him on our most wanted list, but now he'd moved up to the FBI's Most Wanted. Every law enforcement agency all over the country would be after him. I didn't feel one bit sorry for Adams. "You'll get what you deserve, you asswipe. I just hope it's sooner not later," I said to the sky.

I fingered the button on my walkie-talkie. "Argent's out here, Harry. No pulse. And no chance. Head injury."

I heard the sirens coming up the road as my walkie-talkie

crackled. Sounding something like a hundred squad cars squealed to a halt.

"We need to clear the house, Zoe. I'll send some of the troops around to you," said Harry. Then silence for a moment. "Okay, Zoe. Some EMS guys are working on Reed now. And another crew is coming around right now to you and Lonnie."

There was silence for another moment, then Harry said, "The bullet only grazed Reed's leg. He had on a vest so the blood on his shoulder must have come from wiping his hand. I got a feeling he fainted just looking at all his own blood."

"Could have just been the shock of seeing Argent go down that dropped him," I said.

I put my gun away and stayed with Argent until the EMS guys got there. I shook my head at them, but of course they checked anyway.

Three police officers I didn't know joined me. They also didn't know Lonnie Argent, but I could tell they felt the loss of a fellow officer. One burly cop knelt down, made the sign of the cross and offered a prayer. Then the three of them headed out to the barn-like structure when I told them that we thought Adams had had a bike stored out there. "Just secure it until CSU gets here, guys," I said.

"Come on inside this house, Zoe," said Harry's calm voice over the walkie-talkie. "As soon as you can. You ain't gonna believe it."

I walked up the steps to the back door, slipping on latex gloves, then opened the door and stepped into a kitchen. The kitchen was stark and blinding. White floor, white walls and ceiling, white appliances. You'd soon need sunglasses or you'd get a headache. It was unbelievable and unlike anything I'd ever seen.

Harry met me in the kitchen. "All secure?" I nodded. "CSU will chase us out of here in a minute. We need to get our looks in right now." Harry walked to a door with a glass window that opened onto what looked like a laundry room. But when he opened the door there was a small space, like a closet, which Harry said was an airlock. Another glass door let us go into the little laundry room.

CSU will be in here for hours, I thought.

It was a laundry room all right, but it was more than that. The room was sealed off by a second airlock that led into the garage. I opened the door leading into the garage. A black and chrome Yamaha sat there. As I looked at it, I could see why someone would think it was evil-looking. But if the Yamaha was here, what was Adams riding?

I went back into the strange laundry room. It was also all white and stainless steel. At one end was a shower. White smocks and scrubs and booties like doctors wear were folded and stacked on shelves or hung from hooks. A stainless steel apparatus sat on a counter top. A sticker on it read "autoclave."

"Have you ever seen anything like this?" asked Harry.

"No way," I said. "Talk about a weird guy . . . he's high on the weird scale for sure."

A blinding white washer and dryer sat opposite the autoclave and counter. Shelf after shelf held every cleaning and sanitizing product you could imagine: laundry soaps, bleaches, cleansers, sanitizing hand and body soaps, exfoliating creams, loofahs, sponges, deodorants, lotions and moisturizing creams, pumice stones, shaving creams, and disposable razors.

"Everything you could possibly need or want to sterilize and sanitize your body, and, I assume, your clothes," I said.

"There's even magnesia tablets, laxatives to cleanse your

insides," said Harry. "Brr, this place gives me the creeps."

"It's a decontamination room," I said. "Adams must be a germophobic."

"Took lessons from Howard Hughes," Harry said.

"Who? Oh, that billionaire movie mogul guy. The one that movie *The Aviator* is about, huh? Weird guy."

"Yeah, that one," Harry said. "See our generation gap isn't too far apart."

"Loony toons, all right."

The forensic technicians came in. "You guys leaving prints and contaminating the scene?" the tech in charge asked.

"Yeah, we're new to homicide," Harry said. "Left trace all over the place."

"Aww, you've done this before," the technician said. His nametag read Kerzner. He was well-muscled, broad shoulders and a small waist and buns. He had blonde hair and brown eyes, but his best feature was a wonderful smile. The smile lit up his whole face and put a twinkle in his eyes.

"More times than I like to remember." Harry's tone betrayed his weariness.

A young woman technician came out of the hallway that probably led to the bedroom. Her nametag read Tiffany. "An office setup is in here . . . computer, printer, scanner, fax and guess what else?"

"Porno videos and books and DVDs," said Harry.

"You peeked?" She poked him on the shoulder with her fist.

"No, just know the type."

"Tiffany, what's on the computer?" I asked. "Can you check it? Maybe there's something on it to help us find him."

"I can take a quick look if you like." Tiffany had long

natural blonde hair and cornflower blue eyes and walked with a majorette strut that wasn't lost on the guys.

"That would be great if you can," I said. "The more we can learn about this guy, the better chance we'll have to catch him."

Tiffany powered on the computer and booted it up. Her fingers flew over the keys as she typed. "Wow, this guy really *was* freaky."

"Well, we knew that, but what's especially freaky?" I looked at the screen and if I wasn't already prepared for the worst, I might have been shocked. Adams had what looked like hundreds of pornographic photos. I was relieved that no child porn was turning up so far.

Everything graphically filed in anatomically correct files like buns, tits, nasty sluts, then cruder files like clits and pussy and assholes.

When Tiffany next spoke she sounded a bit shell shocked. "He's got chat sessions here that he's saved. He obviously got his jollies by chatting with women."

"A germophobic like Adams probably didn't want to have sex with a real woman."

"Most likely couldn't," said Harry.

"Yeah, nasty women." Tiffany punched more keys. "I need to take this into the lab and download it and try to sort it all out. But this one session here, he's telling this girl 'Lying Eyes' to get a butterfly tattoo," she said.

"Yes, that's definitely stuff we need hard copies of," I said.

"Is he the one who killed the cadet and the other female officers?" Tiffany asked.

"Looks that way," Harry said.

"Then I'll be especially thorough. This scumbag is going to pay," Tiffany said.

A loud commotion came from the laundry room. "Hey, Tiffany, what on earth is this?" A chubby young man, a CSU fingerprint technician, came in to the bedroom. His nametag read "Vince." He held a half-gallon glass fruit jar in his left hand. Inside were jellyfish looking blobs with stringy lines floating in a pinkish liquid.

I took one look and my gag reflex went into overtime for a moment as I realized these were the strips of skin with the butterfly tattoos on them. When I'd calmed my stomach, I said, "You really don't want to know, Vince, but take it back to the lab for positive identification."

Vince and Tiffany looked at me in bewilderment. "Unless I'm way off base, those are skinned-off tattoos of this guy's victims," I said.

A couple of government types were striding up as Harry and I walked outside Warren Adams' house. These two men looked to be cut from the same cookie cutter. Tall, well-muscled, short hair cuts. Charcoal-colored suits and striped neckties and black loafers. Only difference that I could see was maybe ten years in age.

"You the cops Reed and Argent were working with?" the one in front asked. His voice was gruff and authoritative.

"Yes," Harry said.

I could tell Harry wasn't intimidated.

"Where were you when our boys got shot up?" the Fed asked.

"Driving to this location," I said.

"Couldn't you have gotten here sooner?" The older one had gray hair, but his face was unlined, and he would probably look forty-five when he turned eighty-five.

"Couldn't they have waited for backup? It's called standard operating procedure," Harry shot back.

"You are right," the younger of the two said. "They both knew better."

I didn't want to get on the bad side of these agents. They obviously were stunned about their guys. Especially about losing Lonnie Argent. "They may not have had a choice," I said. "Adams probably started shooting."

"Reed can most likely answer these questions to your satisfaction," Harry said. His tone was still sarcastic. The two men ignored him, which had no affect on Harry. Harry then turned to me and said, "Here comes our commander."

Sure enough, Commander Lianne Crowder was getting out of her SUV. "Gentlemen, I need my officers now. We need to get this cop killer off the street. You might want to head over to the hospital and check on your guy."

"Commander we need to debrief them," the older agent said.

"Nothing to debrief," said Harry. "It was all over before we got here."

"We understand, but we need what information you can provide for our records," said the older one.

"We can certainly give you a statement later," I said.

"Not now, gentlemen," said Lianne. "We have a murder suspect to capture."

I could tell the older agent wasn't too happy, but his partner tapped his arm. "She's right. Let's go see how Reed is doing. Maybe we can get some intel from him."

"I want to see Lonnie first. We've been friends since Quantico." The older one headed around the house. The younger agent followed.

Lianne stepped up closer to us and spoke in a husky whisper. "We've got Adams spotted. I don't want those two mucking up our investigation."

"What are we waiting for?" asked Harry. The three of us

began walking towards our vehicles.

"Where is he? And are you riding with us?" I asked Lianne.

"Harry's driving?" Lianne asked.

"Yes, but this time it'll be an advantage," I said.

"You're damn right it will," said Harry. "Get in and we'll discuss this on the way."

We got in the car . . . Lianne and I sort of scrambled for the front seat and I won. She didn't have time to argue. She barely managed to jump in as Harry started the car rolling.

Lianne and I both tightened our seat belts as Harry burned rubber about two hundred yards down the highway. I wished we could be like TV cops in New York and put one of those red bubble lights on the car roof; even a siren would be nice. APD homicide doesn't have them, although there are times when such devices would be welcomed additions.

"Where are we heading?" Harry asked.

"Go north and exit East on Highway 71 and we'll get an update from there," said Lianne.

"The helicopter has him spotted," I said, making a statement instead of a question.

"Yes." Lianne kept talking on her cell. "Damn." She hung up and told Harry to step on it.

"Wha—?" Harry started.

"Harry," I interrupted, "you concentrate on driving. I'll ask the questions. What's going on, Lianne?"

"The Feds are coming to the party too. They're monitoring our dispatch and our chopper."

"Like you said earlier . . . who cares as long as the bastard gets caught," I said.

"I don't think they'll capture," said Lianne.

"Your point being?" said Harry. "Just save the state some money."

"That's not how we do things, Harry," said Lianne.

"That's how I'd do it if I were in charge," Harry said. "A cop killer gets no sympathy from me."

"Not sympathy, Harry," I said. "Doing what's right."

"Did he do what was right?" Harry's voice caught, and I knew then the whole thing was even getting to him, although he'd never admit it.

"If he's killed, it will be their headache, not ours," I said. I remembered the younger agent. "I don't think the Feds will shoot without reason. Despite all their bad press."

"Oh, damn," said Lianne. She listened on her cell phone for a few more seconds. "They've lost him."

"Are you shitting me?" asked Harry.

"What's happened?" I asked.

"He took off across a pasture and into some woods."

In Remembrance:

Sergeant Earl Hall, 50, (March 4, 2002)
Sergeant Earl Hall suffered a fatal heart attack shortly after responding to a burglary alarm in the downtown area of Austin. After determining the call was a false report, Sergeant Hall and his partner returned to the station to attend a meeting. Sergeant Hall collapsed during the meeting and was rushed to a nearby hospital where he died approximately one hour later. Sergeant Hall had been with the Austin Police Department for 21 years.

(Austin City Connection -
The Official Web site of the City of Austin)

Chapter Twenty

We dropped Lianne back at her SUV, and Harry and I headed back to headquarters. The forensics technicians would keep working . . . sorting information, clues, trace, photographing, and doing everything necessary to have as strong a case as possible against Warren Adams.

Two hours later Tiffany, the computer technician from forensics, called me on my office phone. "You were right about the skinned tattoos. And Adams' big sex life was these chat rooms. He'd meet these women online, they'd have cybersex and he'd jack-off."

"Cybersex?"

"Yes, the two of them would meet in a private chat room and type to each other . . . like they were having a conversation in person," Tiffany said. "Then they'd tell each other what they wanted to do to each other sexually. They were very explicit. Afterwards he'd make a file detailing what had been going on, calling them sluts and saying how nasty they were. But then he'd detail all his sexual fantasies and satisfactions. Yet at the end, he kept calling himself *nasty*.

"One minute," she said, "he's telling them what he wants to do to them while in the chat room, then the next minute he calls them every name in the book."

"And meeting them online was for cybersex?" I asked.

"Yep."

"Guess I never knew chat rooms could be so much fun."
My sarcasm was obvious.

"Really," said Tiffany. "I guess we miss out because we
like sex with a real person . . . not a make-believe one."

Tiffany had no way of knowing that my own sex life was
in the make-believe category, but certainly not like Warren
Adams' fantasies. I didn't enlighten her. "Takes all kind," I
said.

"I can do without the perverts of the world." She cleared
her throat. "Adams did suggest to a half dozen women that
they needed to get a butterfly tattoo on their buttocks before he met them. Actually, his suggestion sounded more
like an order. That if they didn't get the tattoo that was the
end of it all. Told them to go to Annie Frannie's Tattoo
Parlor. That he'd pay for it."

"I'll bet that's how he set them up for the kill."

"Right," said Tiffany. "He got them all excited to meet
him in person, set up a meet and then killed them because
they were nasty sluts."

"One of the sickest bastards I've run across," I said.

Tiffany cleared her throat. "I'm e-mailing you this one
chat session. I think if you read it you'll understand more
about what I mean. Print it up and read it, but be
warned . . . it's strong stuff."

"Thanks Tiff, you do good work."

"I also have some good news for you," she said. "You remember Jim and Gary from our department that worked
with you out at Mansfield Dam?"

"Of course. Good guys."

"They've been working out at Adams' house. Jim just
came in here to tell me to tell you he found a scrapbook out
there. Adams' father was a cop over in New Orleans. But he
had to be suspended. He beat two prisoners to death."

"Oh no. Don't tell me Adams senior is the classic child-abuser father," I said.

"We're not sure about dad being an abuser. But two other items from the scrapbook are of interest," Tiffany said. "One is a newspaper clipping about a young female police officer who was murdered by her adopted younger brother, Warren Adams. Adams spent three years in a juvenile detention center. And there's a copy of a social worker's report in which Adams said his sister sexually abused him for years."

"It says adopted younger brother?"

"Yeah."

"He told someone else that his sister was adopted."

"It would have to be that he was the adopted child," said Tiffany. "DNA says Warren Adams is Caucasian and his parents' names are Lena and Raoul Sandol. They were originally from Mexico City. They are both deceased."

"Wonder where the Adams name came from?" I wondered.

"Maybe he made it up . . . thought it sounded good," she said.

"Or maybe he reverted back to his birth name," I said.

"Did he kill them?" I wondered aloud.

"Actually, he was suspected in the death of Lena Sandol but not charged. He and the father then moved from New Orleans to Texas because the sister, Marie Elena Sandol was in Houston," said Tiffany.

"Anything on the father's death?" I asked. "Wonder did he kill Mr. Sandol?"

"I wouldn't doubt it," said Tiffany. "Not for a minute."

Tiffany said she'd call as more information became available.

Harry came in from reporting to Lianne, and I told him

what CSU had found out. Harry's voice was full of disgust. "So abuse was part of the equation?"

"Looks like it. Being adopted and sexually abused changed him into a murdering bastard."

"I have no sympathy for him," Harry said.

"Neither do I, Harry. Neither do I. There comes a time in your adulthood when you must accept responsibility for your actions as a human being."

"Some of these cry babies have no idea what a bad childhood really is like."

"Did you have a bad one, Harry?"

But he only looked at me and didn't answer.

No one went home to stay. I went home long enough to shower, change clothes and to feed Melody and Lyric, who wanted attention, but I drove immediately back to headquarters. It was a long night, going over every scrap of information we had. Trying to come up with an idea as to where our suspect had gone. When dawn broke, we were no closer to finding Adams than when we lost him yesterday. I took a short nap in Lianne's SUV. The seats reclined and I probably slept two hours.

Shortly after I woke up and went back inside, Lianne got a phone call from the hospital. And gave us the word that Anne was going to be okay. But she couldn't talk to anyone yet. We still were not sure who had shot her. It didn't fit Adams' profile but who knew what had gone down.

I was glad to hear Anne would survive and vowed to get over to the hospital to see her as soon as I could. And Harry and I would keep on until we found out who had shot her and see him punished.

While we were chasing Warren Adams, the shooting of Esperanza Ramos, the Alamo City ex-officer who had been shot in her car out at Zilker Park, was solved. Esperanza had a very angry ex-husband who had decided a copycat killing was the best way to take her out. He was on the run, but none of us thought he'd be out of jail for long.

It wasn't until a couple days later that I thought about asking if Esperanza had a blue butterfly tattoo on the butt. By then she'd been cremated.

Harry came in about five thirty a.m. with carryout boxes of breakfast foods he bought at Denny's. He looked fresh and said he'd gone home and showered. He and Lianne and I wolfed down the food along with a fresh pot of coffee that Lianne made.

It was about six thirty a.m. when the patrol car spotted Adams and called dispatch. "Where is he?" asked Harry.

"Headed east on Highway 71," said Lianne.

"How do we know it's Warren Adams?" I asked.

"We don't really have a description of the bike he's riding now," said Harry.

"Do we know for sure what he looks like?" I wondered.

Lianne had already asked those questions of dispatch. She hung up and clued us in. "Adams stopped at a convenience store out on Highway 290 and the clerk behind the counter recognized the photo of him on TV. Fortunately, she played it cool and after he left, she called 911. She got a good look at his motor bike. A little red scooter type like her brother used to have. Says it has a Louisiana license plate on the back."

Lianne called dispatch back. "Get somebody out to that convenience store and pull their video security tape. Let's be one hundred percent sure we got the right guy before we get too excited." She hung up her cell phone only to have it ring again immediately. She listened briefly then hung up once more.

"We're sure enough, let's go," Lianne said. "I'll take my SUV and you two follow me. But stay in radio contact. The chopper is getting up right now."

As we hurried out to our cars, Lianne told us an off-duty deputy from the Travis County Sheriff's office who had a police radio in his car had spotted the red motor scooter with Louisiana plates. He followed it and got close enough to say he was reasonably certain it was Adams.

"He just turned onto Burleson Road," said Lianne.

"He's heading to the academy?" I couldn't help noticing the irony in that. "Is Adams out of his mind?"

"I'm sure his reasons make sense to him," said Lianne.

Harry and I were in his car and communicating with Lianne by walkie-talkie. She had to keep her cell phone line open for all the incoming calls.

Harry followed Lianne onto Burleson Road. He blew the lights at Montopolis and at Smith School Road.

Lianne came back on the radio. "The chopper says Adams has gone inside the main building at APD and the FBI guys are there too."

"Think he'll give up?" I wondered.

"Taking hostages is more like it," said Harry. Three quick turns took us onto the street where the academy is located. "He's not the type to give up."

As we drove into the Academy parking lot, we could see FBI cars and men. There were three agents. The two we had seen earlier at Adams' house and another look-alike type.

Commander Lianne Crowder jumped out before the wheels of her SUV stopped turning. "I want to know who the hell is in charge here?"

"I imagine you are, Commander," said the younger agent. He pulled out his identification badge—Ben

Danvers. We had not met him at Adams' house.

"You're damn right. This is property of the Austin Police Department," Lianne said. She had no intension of giving any ground to these agents.

"A federal agent has been killed and another one wounded," said the older agent. "That makes this federal business and I'm senior officer." He held out his ID and badge, Wayne Barstow. The name fit him somehow . . . tough, strong and red-necked.

"Excuse me, Commander. While you two are seeing who has the brassiest balls," I said, "this guy is inside and may have hostages."

Dispatch came through on our walkie-talkies. "Sergeant Art Torres called from inside, using his cell phone. Two female officers have been taken hostage by Adams. He's barricaded himself and the officers in the Lieutenant's office."

"Where is my SWAT Team?" Lianne demanded.

"Their ETA is . . . they should be there," dispatch told her.

As dispatch spoke, a black van roared into the parking lot. The SWAT Team piled out and began setting up. I felt an icy coldness in my stomach. Byron had been a member of this elite team before he'd been shot. It was hard to watch these guys in action, knowing how my husband had been incapacitated. Harry saw me and grabbed my arm. He pulled me close for a moment and look directly at me. "You okay?"

"I will be when they get this scumbag killer off the streets."

Agent Barstow wasn't happy, but he knew he'd been outnumbered, outmaneuvered and outfoxed with the arrival of the APD Special Team guys.

SWAT quickly got set up and everything was ready for

the negotiator to call Adams on the phone. In the meantime, the remainder of the FBI agents and the police officers took positions around the building. If Adams tried to get out any of the doors, they were all covered.

Harry and I were at the back door with Lianne and two patrol officers. I barely heard the phone ringing inside, but after a moment, I heard two shots ring out.

It wasn't the SWAT guns. Our walkie-talkies crackled. "Hey, you nut. What did you do?" The SWAT commander's frustration clearly came over the radio.

"Who's shooting? I didn't give a shoot order," said Lianne.

"I got him. I got the bastard that killed Lonnie Argent and wounded Craig Reed." I recognized the voice of Barstow. "Those were my guys . . . my team. Lonnie was one of my best friends."

Harry and Lianne and I reached the scene first. Lianne bent down to check Adams. He was dressed in black motorcycle skintight clothing, with black boots and a black leather jacket. He didn't have a helmet. Guess he'd only had the one left in his garage at his house.

"He's dead," said Lianne. "Let me have your gun, Barstow."

I stood looking at the young man whose eyes stared up at the sky and the young man I had shot a few months ago came unbidden to my mind . . . Would I forever see those dead eyes in my dreams? Why do these guys think they are invincible? Don't they realize this is not a movie or a game? Do they just think once they are down they can just get up and walk away?

"It was a good shoot, Commander. Adams was climbing out that window. I saw it all," said Danvers. "He fired his weapon at us."

I breathed a sigh of relief that I had not been the shooter. Not this time.

"Doesn't matter," said Barstow. "Asshole's dead."

Somehow, I felt cheated. It was over much too soon. I'm glad I didn't shoot him, but I wanted to go over and kick the SOB.

In Remembrance:

Officer Amy Donovan, 37, (October 31, 2004) Officer Donovan was killed when she was accidentally struck by a police cruiser during a foot chase. At approximately 10:48 p.m., Officer Donovan and a fellow officer observed a suspicious person in the 1300 block of Poquito Street. Officer Donovan began a foot chase of the suspect and her fellow officer followed in a patrol unit. During the chase, the patrol car struck Officer Donovan. Officer Donovan later died as a result of her injuries. Officer Donovan was in her fifth month of service as a commissioned officer of the Austin Police Department at the time of her death.

(Austin City Connection -
The Official Web site of the City of Austin)

Chapter Twenty-One

◆ ◆ ◆

"Did you read all the printouts from Adams' computer?" I leaned back in my chair and looked at Harry.

"No way. He was a jerk, and I have no desire to waste my time."

"His abusive father drank himself to death. His mother drove him crazy so he killed her. Supposedly, he burned their house down and she died in the fire. Then he killed his cop sister because she suspected he'd killed their mother."

"I thought he killed her because she sexually abused him." Harry pretended non-interest.

"That may have only been a boy's fantasy," I said. "His adopted sister was beautiful, and I'm sure he lived in a constant wet dream fantasy with his sister as the star."

I patted Harry's shoulder. "I'm going to read some of this to Byron. We still don't know how much he understands."

We discussed the status of Anne Panzarella's case. We were certain Adams had shot her. When Anne was out of recovery and able to talk, she told us a male on a Yamaha shot her. She had gone to that east side area to settle down a gang rumble and had started home.

"I saw this guy on a motorcycle run a red light," she said. "I stopped him and was calling in his license plate, but he took off before I got an answer back. I lost him, then he laid in wait for me, and when I got close . . . he came out of nowhere and shot me."

When we checked with dispatch, the license matched Adam's Yamaha. But we never found a handgun in any of his belongings or in his house. We're fairly certain he ditched that gun. Since he was dead, we closed the case.

"Did you hear Anne was going to retire?" I asked Harry.

"I'd heard a rumor," he said. "I don't blame her. Her full recovery is going to take some time."

Harry had surprised me when he came with me to see my husband. When I first began working with Harry, he mentioned he'd known Byron slightly. Then later he said they'd worked together on a big fraud case. After we'd wrapped up our report on Adams, Harry asked me to join him for dinner. I said I wanted to go see Byron first, and Harry insisted on coming with me.

"I've gone to see him a couple of times since that case we worked on last year."

I told him I didn't know that, and Harry said he didn't want to tell me in case I thought he was being ghoulish. "I know better." So we drove out to Golden Acres together in my car with me driving.

"Any news on that Swedish doctor?"

"Nothing yet."

"And the guardianship?"

"My attorney assures me it will go through without any problems." I brushed Byron's hair back and reminded myself to call his barber in for a haircut. "As long as Jean stays out of it. But I think she will. Levi's keeping a tight rein on her right about now, I think."

"So Adams got off on cybersex because he didn't want to get germs," I said. "And he set up women who looked like the sister but first made sure they had a butterfly tattoo on their buttocks."

"Guess it takes all kinds," Harry said, as he walked over to the window and looked out. "You ready to go get some food?"

"I thought you'd never ask."

Harry walked out so I could tell my husband goodbye in private. I gave Byron a kiss and walked out, trying without success to hold back the tears.

When I reached my car, Harry met me and his arms encircled me, holding me tight. "Don't give up all hope." He kissed my forehead.

"How did you know I was hurting?" I asked as I fastened my seatbelt.

Harry's pager went off, then mine began beeping.

"Oh no," I said. "I'm so hungry."

"Time to rock and roll, Zoe. The asswipes don't pay any attention to the dinner hour. We'll grab a burger later."

I groaned, started my car and headed north towards the new crime scene.

Author's Notes

Homicide: Unsolved Cases of APD

Throughout history, the unlawful taking of a human life has ranked as the most serious of crimes. Within our legal system, the crime of murder has no statute of limitations, meaning that a killer may always be brought to justice regardless of how many years have passed since the crime was committed.

Homicide investigators see the job of bringing these killers to justice as a solemn duty. They realize that justice is owed not only to the deceased victim, but to the family and friends left behind; those living victims who require closure of a case to begin the healing process. The safety of the community and the sanctity of human life also require that justice be served. In the words of ex-NYPD Homicide detective and well-known instructor Vernon Geberth, "We work for God."

A homicide case is considered closed when a suspect has been identified, charged, and arrested. In the case files of the Austin Police Department's Homicide Unit, 127 cases are still waiting for closure. These "cold cases," some dating back to the 1960s, lack the critical information or evidence needed to identify or charge a suspect. In an additional 35 cases, a suspect has been identified and charged, but not located for arrest.

Declining rates of violent crime in Austin have lowered the Homicide Unit's caseload, providing an opportunity to reassign personnel to cold cases. The Cold Case Homicide Unit is assigned five detectives and a sergeant to work full time on cold cases. Now is an opportune time to reexamine cold cases for several reasons: Advances in forensic analysis of evidence, such as DNA, may yield new clues or establish links to suspects that were not possible in the past. Over time, alliances between suspects and witnesses may have diminished, removing the reluctance of those with knowledge of the crime to cooperate with investigators.

The killers themselves may have lowered their guard over time, leading them to confide information to others or come out of hiding. Investigators know that most homicide cases are closed within the first twenty-four to forty-eight hours. In fact, APD's Homicide Unit has maintained a very high closure rate (100 percent in 1999). However, when this critical window of opportunity slides shut and no lead has developed, investigators must often rely on the public coming forward with information that will reestablish a direction in a case. This is why the Austin Police Department is providing information on cold cases to the public. Investigators hope that someone reading about these cases will recognize and come forward with that critical information.

Criminologists estimate that in 84 percent of cold cases, the killer's name is already written down somewhere in the case file within the first 30 days. New information may draw a line to that name.

(Austin City Connection -
The Official Web site of the City of Austin)

About the Author

◆　◆　◆

Double-award winner, Jan Grape's *Austin City Blue* (Five Star Publishing) was a 2002 nominee for an Anthony Award for Best First Novel of 2001. *Austin City Blue* was reprinted as a paperback from WorldWide, and Recorded Books brought out an unabridged audio book. *Found Dead In Texas*, a short story collection was also published by Five Star Publishing. Jan received a "Friends of PWA" award in 2002, a special Shamus given by the Private-Eye Writers of America. She also won an Anthony for Best Short Story and a Macavity Award for Best Non-Fiction, and has been nominated for an Edgar, an Agatha and a Shamus. Many of her stories have been reprinted in Japan, and she's published numerous articles and interviews. For over sixteen years, Jan was a regular columnist for *Mystery Scene Magazine*. Jan's held offices and/or membership in Mystery Writers of America-Southwest, Private-Eye Writers of America, American and International Crime Writers, and is a co-founder/ life member of Heart of Texas Chapter/Sisters-in-Crime. Jan and her husband Elmer sold Mysteries & More bookstore in Austin, TX, to spend more time with their five grandchildren and to travel, and they now live in a RV full-time with their black cats, Nick and Nora.